The Way to
RIO LUNA

The Way to
RIO LUNA

ZORAIDA CÓRDOVA

Scholastic Press | New York

Library of Congress Cataloging-in-Publication Data available

ISBN 978-1-338-23954-6

10 9 8 7 6 5 4 3 2 1   20 21 22 23 24

Printed in the U.S.A.   23

First edition, June 2020

Book design by Keirsten Geise

FOR ADRIAN MEDINA

← 1 →

The Boy
Who Believed

DANNY MONTEVERDE BELIEVED.

He believed in making wishes, and in lucky four-leaf clovers, and in underground tunnels that lead to wondrous places. He knew if he could reach the second star to the right and go straight on till morning, he'd be well on his way to Neverland, just like the kids in *Peter Pan*. And if he stood in the right place, at the right time, he could travel through a moon portal. Danny knew that just because some things couldn't be seen or explained, it didn't mean they couldn't be real. Magic was everywhere, if you just paid attention.

He'd learned to believe from his sister, Pili, and she'd learned from her favorite book of fairy tales, *The Way to Rio Luna* by Ella St. Clay. For as long as Danny could remember, it'd been just the two of them. While their foster homes and orphanages and schools always changed, Danny could count on two things: his sister and their book. Pili had bought the copy with her own money at a yard sale. It was the only thing she'd ever owned, paid for with the few dollars she'd been given for doing other kids' chores. The paper was frayed and nearly falling apart because every night, without fail, Pili would read to her little brother.

They hid under alcoves, in tiny rooms under the stairs, inside closets—anywhere two small kids could fit and not be noticed. Even when it was cold, or they could hear their foster parents fighting, or when their new guardian forgot to feed them, Danny and Pili could always escape into a world of magical forests, enchanted gardens, and shooting stars. Each story took them to a new part of their favorite fairyland. Danny particularly loved the ones set at the heart of the world, the place called Rio Luna. There a great river was home to fairies, silver trees, and extraordinary magic.

"I promise, Danny," Pili told him. It was his ninth birthday, and she'd found enough change to buy him a chocolate–peanut butter cupcake with sprinkles. "One day, we're going to find a place that's better than here."

"Like how Heidi from Mrs. Murphy's class and her family go to Hawaii?" he asked, licking frosting off his fingertips.

Pili laugh-snorted. "Even better." She took his pinky finger with hers. "When we get to Rio Luna, we can have our own rooms. We can eat whatever we want. No one will hurt us or try to separate us. We'll be able to fly with shooting stars and have tea with witches. We'll be free. I promise."

But a few days after making that promise, Danny was placed in the care of a family called the Finnegans while Pili stayed at the group home. Before Danny left, Pili let him take *The Way to Rio Luna*.

"This is only temporary. We'll be together again soon," she told him, and Danny took her pinky in his and didn't let go until his social worker, Mrs. Contreras, beeped the car horn.

A few days later, Danny received the news that Pili was gone. There was no trace of her. Not her backpack or clothes or toothbrush or her favorite hair ribbon. It was as if she vanished into thin air. The police and social workers told Danny that Pili was a runaway, but he knew his sister wouldn't leave him behind. They had pinky sworn, and that kind of promise was unbreakable. There had to be some sort of explanation. Pili was out there somewhere, searching for the place they'd talked about together. He would find her.

That's how Danny Monteverde became one of the world's strongest believers in magic.

←2→

The Boy Who Tried to Fly

ONE MONTH AFTER PILI'S unexpected disappearance, Danny still believed.

He believed in magic and in the stories that kept him awake in the middle of the night. That was how he was going to find Pili in Rio Luna.

He was going to fly.

His new foster family, the Finnegans, seemed nice enough if you only looked at the photos on the fireplace mantel—a mother, a father, and two kids of their own. But after a month of living with them, Danny got to know a different side of the perfect home. The Boy Finnegan didn't like the way Danny ate everything on his dinner plate, even the smelly cauliflower, because then Mother Finnegan said, "Why can't you be more like *Danny*?" The Girl Finnegan thought Danny's nose was too big for his small, square face and often made fun of him for it. Mother Finnegan didn't quite know what to do with a child who grew so quickly. Danny's hair was thick and wavy like ropes of black licorice. It needed a trim nearly every week, and soon enough, she stopped cutting it. Danny couldn't fit into the boy's hand-me-downs, either, so his pants and sleeves always showed an inch of his thin ankles and wrists. Father Finnegan didn't like that Danny would rather stay cooped up in the corner of the living room with a book. He wanted Danny to like things like throwing and kicking balls around.

But Danny preferred books. He carried Pili's copy of *The Way to Rio Luna* by Ella St. Clay everywhere he went. When he wasn't picked for the school play, he'd read it in the auditorium. While his foster siblings had soccer practice, Danny always managed to find a quiet corner high up on the bleachers. He'd read at the mall food court while the Finnegans spent hours and hours shopping for clothes and toys. That always meant Danny would get new hand-me-downs soon, which he didn't mind. The only thing Mother Finnegan had offered to buy for Danny was a new copy to replace his tattered book.

Unfortunately, *The Way to Rio Luna* was out of print everywhere. Even if he could find a shiny new one, Danny wouldn't want it. It wouldn't feel right. This one was Pili's. On the cover was a secret garden with floating fairies between spindly trees. Arrows and a compass rose surrounded the title and the author's name. There were rips and creases on the jacket, but it was nothing a bit of tape couldn't fix. The words on the yellowing paper reminded him of the impossible—of the people in his life who were long gone. Sometimes, the book felt alive.

One time, he thought that he could see the letters on the page glowing. When he told Mother Finnegan about it, she said his imagination was too active. Danny didn't feel very active. In fact, one of his favorite things was *sitting*, which was the opposite of being active. He could sit and read for hours and hours. He loved that the words on the page came to life in his mind, like blobs of watercolor taking shape.

But reading alone wasn't the same as reading with Pili. He missed the way she did all the voices, like the one of the Moon Witch who lived inside a tree. He missed the way she could always distract him when the house was full of scream-ing and slamming doors. He missed the peanut butter and jelly sandwiches she'd sneak him before bed. She'd put Cap'n Crunch into the peanut butter so it would taste extra sweet and be extra crunchy. He clung to those memories of her the way he clung to his book. There was only one thing Danny believed in more than magic, and it was that Pili loved him and would never have left him alone on purpose.

He knew he'd find her waiting for him in Rio Luna. He simply needed to figure out how to get there. So he looked for portals in the backs of wardrobes. He even dug a hole in the Finnegans' backyard. But instead of a rabbit hole, he discovered only a septic tank. Danny tried to apologize, but when he went to find his foster parents, he overhead them speaking about him.

"We had to pick the looniest of the bunch, didn't we?" Father Finnegan said. "Other kids read the same drivel and they don't act this way."

Mother Finnegan made a clucking noise, like the neigh-bor's chicken. "Hush now. He just needs time. After his sister—"

"He's got a new sister and a new brother," Father Finnegan said, cutting her off. "The kid doesn't even try. In the morning,

I'm going to throw that book of his in the trash before he breaks a mirror trying to get to La La Land."

Danny didn't listen to the rest. He went right to his narrow twin bed, fished out *The Way to Rio Luna* from under the covers, and hid it on a dusty shelf in the garage.

He hoped Father Finnegan would forget about it, and for a few days he did.

But then Father Finnegan surprised Danny and his foster siblings with a fishing trip. Danny had always wanted to go on a boat and imagine what a pirate might have felt like. But then Danny remembered that all the fishing supplies were in the garage, gathering dust from the winter. Before he had time to act, Father Finnegan found *The Way to Rio Luna* next to the box of fishing wire and hooks.

"What's this?" Father Finnegan snatched up the book in his calloused fist.

Danny's heart thundered against his rib cage. He lunged for *The Way to Rio Luna*, but the man was too tall and held the copy up in the air. "It's just a book. It's *my* book, please."

"You have to be part of the real world, Danny," his foster father said, deep lines crinkling his freckled brow. "This is what puts crazy ideas in your head."

"Don't call me that," Danny said, but it was just a

whisper. It was as if his voice was being turned off completely. His body shook as he waited to see what Father Finnegan would do next.

"Get in the car," Father Finnegan said.

Danny filed in and ignored his foster siblings snickering. The girl said, "You're in *trouble.*"

Then Danny watched as Father Finnegan strode past the car and to the row of garbage cans. Before he could think, Danny bolted out of the car and ran down the driveway.

"Please, don't!" Danny shouted. "Please, it's the only thing I have left—"

Father Finnegan held the book out of reach. He opened the lid to the metal garbage can. Danny jumped and reached and grabbed for it. He felt like a mad, wild whirlwind. Tears ran down his face.

"It's for your own good," Father Finnegan said, and he dropped the book into the trash.

Danny cried the entire way to the lake, and while he held his fishing pole. Girl Finnegan blamed his tears for scaring away the fish. They didn't catch a single one. By the time they were ready to go back to the house, Danny's eyes felt puffy and burned when he blinked.

Perhaps it was seeing Danny's hurt, but Father Finnegan relented.

"Fine, if you're going to be hysterical," he said, and marched to the row of garbage cans. He wrenched the lid open, and Danny's insides felt like a sputtering candle. The light blew out when they both realized that the cans were empty. It was trash day.

The Way to Rio Luna by Ella St. Clay, the only thing he had left of his sister, was long gone.

Mother Finnegan clucked around like an apologetic hen. She went to three bookstores, but Danny reminded her that it was out of print. He visited to the library, but none of the local branches carried it. It was as if the book had never existed.

But Danny remembered the stories. He tried to write them down from memory, but they never felt quite the same. Nothing would ever be the same.

———

When Danny decided to climb out the window and stand on the Finnegans' roof, everyone blamed the stories about children flying on shadows and grabbing the tails of shooting stars.

Earlier that same day, Danny had been following the Finnegan kids back home from school (they didn't much like walking *next* to him) when they passed a yard sale. He'd rummaged through the books, but the owner of the house only seemed to read books about serial killers. Then Danny noticed something better. In a bin of old unwanted doll parts and gravy boats was a jar labeled FAIRY DUST. It was only fifty cents, and as he frantically dug into his pocket, Danny discovered he had exactly fifty cents!

Danny had read all kinds of fairy tales and knew how rare and special fairy dust was. It didn't matter if no one else believed him. Magic was real and it would lead him to Pili. He would prove it with his little bottle of yard sale fairy dust.

When night fell and everyone in the Finnegan home had gone to sleep, Danny found his way out onto the roof. He held the small bottle against his heart. Just a sprinkle of the glittering powder would do, and he could be well on his way. It didn't matter that he was an orphan who never quite *fit* into the puzzles of families he was shoved into. The place where he was going was full of orphans just like him. Pili would be there, too.

Danny stood on the rooftop. He could hear crickets and the hoot of an owl, and from the room inside, the soft snores of a family who would be relieved in the morning when he wasn't there.

The moon was full, and so big it looked like it had been pulled closer to the earth by a lasso. Everyone said that if you looked at the moon, you could see a face. Danny did not see a face, no matter how long he stared. Maybe when he got closer, he'd be able to figure it out. He searched for the second star, but there were so many out there. How was he going to find the right one? It was like staring into a field of fireflies, twinkling and blinking and vanishing and reappearing. Before he could panic, he picked the biggest one, closest to the moon. He uncorked the glass vial. He turned the tube over his head and let the fairy dust fall over his hair.

Then he waited.

He waited for a feeling. Something that said, *You can fly!*

He waited for a long time.

So long that the stars even started to shift and move positions, and he had to search for the second star all over again. But the feeling never came. Danny was sure that when someone was sprinkled with fairy dust, they glowed with magic. They glowed like a star themselves. He just needed to believe harder.

So he closed his eyes and took several steps back. He focused on the stars in the sky, and the bulbous moon, and the dust that tickled his scalp and skin. He thought of Pili.

Danny broke into a run and he jumped.

←3→

The Very Lost Boy

EVEN WHEN HIS ARM was bandaged and broken in three places, Danny believed.

The Finnegans took him to the hospital, but he knew he was *really* in trouble when Mrs. Contreras came to see him. Everywhere he turned, adults surrounded him like giants, asking, "Danilo Monteverde! What were you thinking?"

Danny hated when they used his full name. Only Pili was allowed to call him that, and she wasn't here. To everyone else he was simply Danny. The problem with being small and nine years old and alone was that no one listened to him. But he couldn't lie. Pili taught him to always tell the truth.

He said, "I was trying to find her."

Mrs. Contreras had been Danny's social worker for years. She had thick, curly hair that was brown as tree bark, and skin like fresh coffee with steamed milk. She'd never had any kids but said all those she cared for were like her own. Danny always wanted to ask, "Then why don't you adopt us?" But there were so many of them. Danny had once tried to count how many kids had been in his group home, but it was like counting grains of sand or blades of grass. He'd trip up on the numbers and have to start over. The grown-ups called it the System. He hated the way that sounded. It was like he was being sent to a dark, terrible part of a hospital with no windows or doors. *The System.*

"Oh, Danny," Mrs. Contreras said. That's all she said. He recognized how tired her voice sounded, and suddenly he felt terrible. He didn't like the sadness in her big brown eyes, but he hated that no one believed him about Pili even more. "How could you possibly find her this way?"

"That's the way fairy dust works," Danny explained. He tried not to move or his arm felt like there were needles inside. "In the book, the kids really believe. Something must have gone wrong."

"And where would this fairy dust have taken you?" Mrs. Contreras asked.

"Rio Luna. That's where Pili promised we would go together."

"Sweetie, I know you miss your sister," Mrs. Contreras said. When she sighed, she deflated like a party balloon. "But you can't keep doing things like this or you're going to get seriously hurt. You promised me you'd be good."

He'd also made a promise to his sister that he wouldn't forget. How could he do both?

"I know, but—you don't understand," Danny said.

Why couldn't they see that Danny was trying to find Pili? She was out there. People didn't just vanish into thin air. Not unless they had the help of the magic from the stories.

"I'm sorry, Danny, but this is just glitter. It is great that you love these books so much, but they only live on the page. There are no gateways inside closets, and you can't break another mirror trying to find a portal. I want to find you a good family, but I need your help."

Danny didn't want to listen. He tried to turn over on his

hospital bed, but he couldn't because his arm hurt too much. He was forced to keep looking into Mrs. Contreras's face. He was used to this routine. He and Pili had been in more foster homes than he could count. Each time, they had tried to hope to become part of a family, but somehow it never worked out.

How could he be part of a family without his sister? Why did everyone want him to forget?

Mrs. Contreras kept talking. She had tears in her eyes. He wasn't used to seeing grown-ups cry, but Mrs. Contreras sometimes did when she talked about Pili. "We've done everything we can, Danny. But she's gone. It's been months now. The police say she must've run away with the older foster kids."

"She wouldn't leave without me," Danny said. There was a heavy sensation on his chest, like he couldn't breathe easily. "We were supposed to go there together!"

"Is there anywhere else she might have gone?" Mrs. Contreras asked him. "If you tell us a real place, maybe we can search again."

Rio Luna is a real place, Danny thought. But he didn't say it out loud again because he'd already told them. He told the social workers and he told the detective and he told everyone who asked. That was the only place Pili could have gone. Each time, they wrote things down about him. They asked him question after question. They called it an assessment. But Danny knew they were treating him like a broken toy they didn't know how to fix.

Danny shook his head. "There's nowhere else I can think of."

"Try and get some sleep," Mrs. Contreras told him, resigned to his silence. "I'll take this with me." She took his copy of *Peter Pan*, which they'd been assigned at school that week, and Danny knew he wouldn't be getting it back.

He also knew he wasn't going back to the Finnegans'. He'd go with Mrs. Contreras to the group home. But this time, there'd be no Pili to stop the big kids from stealing his socks or to talk to after he woke up from a nightmare.

Sometimes Danny wondered if he'd ever find a family to belong to. What if the parents who had died and the sister who vanished, what if that was the only chance he was going to get? He was a boy who came from nowhere and belonged to no one.

No, Danny thought. *I belong somewhere. I belong with Pili.*

So he let that thought fill his heart, like a tiny, secret star only he could see.

←4→

The Boy Who Fell to Earth

DANNY STILL BELIEVED. BUT for the next couple of years, he kept his feet planted on the ground.

After the Finnegans, he'd moved back into the group home. There were so many kids there that he found it easy to hide and do what he did best: dream up his favorite fairy tales.

But he was tired of being passed around group homes. Of not having a family. His record came with a long list of hospital visits and wild stories, and no one seemed to want a little boy who didn't follow the rules. It was time to stop talking about fairy dust and other realms.

As luck would have it, Mrs. Contreras found a family for him a few days after his tenth birthday. The Haydenson family was very kind. The father was tall, with dark hair and brown skin. The mother had hair the color of red apples and was so short, she and Danny almost stood eye to eye. At first, Danny thought he looked like he could belong to them.

He promised Mrs. Contreras. This time there would be no jumping off roofs or digging holes in the backyard, trying to find a secret passage to a magic world. This time, Danny would be good.

He said please and thank you. He washed his hands after using the bathroom. He helped with laundry and raking the leaves and shoveling snow. Instead of going into the fairy-tale section of the library hoping to find a copy of his book, he wandered to the science section. The Haydensons loved visiting museums and going to plays. Maybe if he was smarter, if he knew facts and art and history, he could be just like them.

Yet no matter how hard he tried to deny it, the world around him tried to insist that magic was real. Shadows played tricks on him. They moved at the corners of his eyes.

One time, he thought he saw one float right in front of him on the way to school, but Mrs. Haydenson told him it must have been a cloud. Danny didn't think a cloud's shadow could look like a person, but he kept this to himself. Some nights, he had fitful dreams about Pili. She was in a dark forest and called out to him, but he always woke up before he understood what she was saying.

One afternoon during spring break, Mrs. Haydenson asked Danny to accompany her to the library. She went straight for books about babies. Danny picked up a book on space with color photos of planets and found a couch where he could read. He read about how stars were big balls of gas that had exploded. In fairy tales, stars could come down to Earth and help you travel across worlds. How could a ball of gas a billion miles away in space be able to do that? Were stars not magical at all? He thought of his favorite Ella St. Clay story, about a guinea pig who catches the tail of a star and uses it to get to a place called the Cliffs of Nowhere. Danny had never met a talking guinea pig, so that must mean that the traveling stars weren't real, either.

Suddenly, it dawned on him. What about the other stories by Ella St. Clay? The one about a young witch who discovered a crack in the air and found herself in the Red

Woods, where she lived with the royal family of jackalopes. Danny searched through a stack of books for proof that there was such a creature as a jackalope—a hare or rabbit with great big antlers. But he couldn't find any evidence that jackalopes existed. It was one thing to leave the stories in the past. It was another to know that they were never true.

He closed his eyes and watched the stories unravel in his mind like bright bursts of color. If these stories weren't real, then what did that mean for Pili?

Danny shut his science books. Heat pricked at his eyes and his mind felt like Mrs. Haydenson's ribbon drawer. Everything was so tangled up. He wished he could talk to someone. Pili. He needed her to make sense of the world around him. He knew he'd made a promise to believe. But now, he was forgetting exactly *what* he was believing in.

"I need you, Pili," Danny whispered to himself.

His corner of the library was quiet. Only the hum of the blasting air conditioner vibrated in the air. He felt his breath catch when there was a flash of movement in the corner of his eye. Dark wisps moved in the air. His heart raced. There was someone standing at the end of the corridor. He couldn't see anything else but a girl-shaped shadow. A light giggle that sent a jolt of lightning to his chest. He knew that laugh anywhere.

"Pili?" he said again. This time his voice was stronger. He made to run after her but tripped over his stack of books.

When he righted himself, the shape was gone. Had there been someone there or had it been his imagination again? Mrs. Contreras had reminded him that sometimes kids, especially lonely kids like Danny, wanted to believe in something so much that their minds played tricks on them. Was that what was happening to him? His own mind was one big trick? He hated that thought.

Then the squeaky feedback of the speakers made his ears hurt.

"The library will be closing in fifteen minutes," a voice said.

Danny hurried between the shelves to return the books he'd been reading. For a moment, a dark blurry figure caught his attention again. Danny shut his eyes and counted backward from ten. When he peeked, the shadows against the wall had begun to move. It reminded Danny of the time he was in art class and dropped a bit of ink in a water cup. The black unfurled and billowed. It was unlike any shadow Danny had ever seen. He remembered that it wasn't just stars that could take you to another realm. Shadows could, too, as long as they were enchanted. He leapt against the wall, his hands ready to close on the dark moving shape.

Pain splintered up his hands and shoulders from slamming into the wall.

"My word!" the librarian, Mr. Dussek, muttered as he walked around the corner. "What *are* you doing, Danny?"

Danny looked up at the wall behind Mr. Dussek. There was nothing there but paint and posters of famous people telling kids to read.

"Just clumsy," Danny said, and picked up the mess of books he'd knocked over.

He convinced himself that the shadows hadn't moved and the blurry shape must've been the librarian passing by. That's what happened when he thought about magic. He forgot what was real and what was fake. Stars were gas, not transportation. Shadows did not move on their own; it was a trick of the light. Everything had a really real, magic-less explanation.

"Are you okay, Danny?" Mrs. Haydenson asked him during dinner that night. Mr. Haydenson was working late again. "You've been quiet since we left the library."

Danny pushed his rice around the plate. He hadn't been able to forget the moving shadow, but he was going to keep his promise to Mrs. Contreras. He was turning eleven in six months, after all. If years in the System had taught him anything, it was that once you hit your teenage years, you didn't believe in anything, anyway. You started scowling and yelling and listening to punk rock music. Danny couldn't imagine himself like that.

"Nothing, I'm just hungry." Danny scooped up his rice and shredded pork and ate faster.

Mrs. Haydenson laughed and patted her belly to show she was full. "Me too, kiddo."

A few weeks later, Mrs. Contreras came to bring Danny back to the group home. The Haydensons hugged him and said they were sorry and they cried, but then let him go anyway. Danny didn't understand why. He'd done everything right. He'd been good and stayed out of trouble. He'd gotten good grades and was one of the best students in his class. He did what everyone had asked him to and it didn't work. What else could he possibly do to find a family that wanted him?

As they rode back in the car, Mrs. Contreras finally explained to him that the Haydensons were going to have triplets and had changed their mind about keeping Danny.

It hurt the most because Danny knew he would make an excellent big brother.

He looked out the car window. It was daylight and kids were playing on the street. There was a girl with long black hair who looked just like Pili. He knew it wasn't her but his insides felt like knots. Then he wondered—could he do what she'd done and run away?

That was the moment Danny could feel everything changing, like the turn of the planets and the seasons and all the things that couldn't be controlled. *He* was changing. Danny, the boy who believed, was ready to grow up.

←5→

The Boy Who Tried to Grow Up

Growing up didn't help Danny fit in with his new foster family, the Garners.

The Garners were his twelfth foster family overall, including the ones he'd shared with Pili. It felt like he could divide his eleven-year-old life into two sections: Before Pili Left and After Pili Left. Before Pili Left was a whirlwind of stories. Of fairyland magic. Of promises and wishes. Without her, *after* her, the world felt drained of color. It was like living somewhere permanently cloudy and gray. It had only gotten worse after his book had been thrown into the trash.

He tried to start fresh with this new family, but he simply didn't have anything in common with the Garners. Though, as bad as they were, Danny knew they could be worse. Mrs. Contreras remained hopeful that Danny would find a permanent home. He didn't believe the Garners would be it, but they were *a* family. So even when Freddy and Teddy were mean, even when they hid his schoolbooks in places he couldn't reach, even when Mr. Garner was red with anger and shouted and Mrs. Garner pretended like nothing was wrong, Danny made it work.

On the morning of a school field trip, Danny woke from a fitful dream. He'd been alone in the dark, surrounded by shadows and whispers. Then someone called out to him from a great, long distance. He didn't recognize the voice because it sounded like the echo after a bell. He rubbed tired, blurry eyes and told himself it was just a dream.

The smells of breakfast wafted up the steps and into the open door of his bedroom. His foster mother must've been in there because the curtains were spread open and let in the orange glow of sunrise. Danny shot up in bed. Another ten minutes and he would have overslept. Mr. Garner liked to wake everyone up at the crack of dawn with him. Danny didn't mind, especially today. But before he got out of bed, he had to make sure it was safe.

Danny peered around the room he shared with Freddy and Teddy. He had to be *very* careful with Freddy and Teddy because they liked pranks more than anything in the world, even more than bacon. Sometimes he woke up with roaches all over his bed. They were plastic, of course. But that is hard to tell when you first wake up and see dozens of bugs covering every inch of your comforter. Freddy and Teddy knew Danny *hated* bugs. He tried to tell Mr. and Mrs. Garner, but they wouldn't listen. Mr. Garner said it was just good fun, and Mrs. Garner smiled in that strange way of hers, like she really wanted to be somewhere else.

Another time, Danny woke up to find his ankles tied with Mrs. Garner's craft ribbon. When he tried to get out of bed, he tumbled right over and fell on his funny bone. There had never been and would never be anything funny about a funny bone. He told Mr. and Mrs. Garner again. Mr. Garner said, "Boys will be boys! Join the fun." But Danny didn't think that was how boys were supposed to act, and there was nothing fun about hurting someone on purpose. After all, Danny and the twins were the same age—eleven. And

Danny didn't act like them. Meanwhile, Mrs. Garner smiled her faraway smile, and Danny learned to keep quiet.

That morning Danny stretched his feet first. No ribbon.

He looked around his bedsheets. No plastic bugs.

He looked on the floor. (One time they shined it with Vaseline so Danny would slip when he took his first step.) The coast was clear.

It made Danny suspicious.

"Danny!" Mrs. Garner called from downstairs. "Breakfast is ready."

"I'll be right down!" He got dressed quickly. As always, his pants were too short, so an inch of his mismatched socks showed. Danny couldn't stop growing. Every day he was sprouting like a beanstalk. Even his hair was getting long again, black locks curled at the ends around his ears. Freddy and Teddy liked to make fun of his hair. But when he asked for new clothes or a haircut, Mr. Garner asked, "Do you think money grows on trees?"

Danny tucked his hair behind his ears and looked at his reflection. His heart gave a squeeze as he shut his eyes and pictured Pili Monteverde's smiling face. The image of her was beginning to grow fuzzy, like a fading photograph, but he could never forget her eyes or smile, because they were the same as his. If Pili were here, she'd put Freddy and Teddy in their place and they'd never bother him again. It was strange, how good memories could make him the saddest.

Maybe it was because he was missing his sister extra that day, or because he was rarely alone in the bedroom he shared with the twins, but Danny placed his fingers against the glass of the wall mirror. He pressed until there was a clear smudge of his fingerprints. For a moment, he imagined that the glass would give way under his touch. Maybe it would ripple. Maybe it would shine with a bright light. Maybe he'd feel a chill as he passed right through it and into another dimension far, far away. Wonderland. The Enchanted Forest. Anywhere.

"Danny!" Mr. Garner yelled. "Don't make me come get you."

He sighed long and hard. Nope, there was no magic in that mirror, just like every other mirror he'd ever tested in his life.

Then he filled up his backpack with what he called his survival kit for field trips: his permission slip, a small bottle of antibacterial gel, extra socks, a sweater, a notebook, a bag of pens, his homework in case Freddy tried to use it as a coaster again, his library card, the chocolate bars he kept hidden from the twins, his space-themed metal lunch box with all his most precious things inside, and the money he made from helping the neighbor pull weeds from her lawn.

He slung his backpack over one shoulder and raced down the steps. The kitchen smelled like bacon and sweet butter and the car grease that was always stuck under Mr. Garner's fingernails. He was a mechanic every day of the week except for Sunday, when he spent the day shouting at the New York Rangers and drinking from brown glass bottles. There were bags and bags of them in the garage. At the end of the week, the recycling truck picked them up and they clinked and clanked so loudly that the whole neighborhood could hear it.

"Good morning," Danny said to the room.

Mrs. Garner was already flipping pancakes onto Danny's plate. Her eyes were tired and sagged like tea bags, but she still smiled warmly at him. She pressed her hand on his head and mussed up his soft curls. At least she appreciated him.

"What's good about it?" Mr. Garner muttered.

"Yeah," Freddy said, mimicking his dad's voice. The twins even wore cream-and-orange baseball jerseys to match their dad. "What's good about it?"

"Yeah," Teddy repeated. "The Giants are *losing* again."

Danny wasn't sure which giants they were talking about. The only giants he knew were in the books he used to read. He thought about saying as much, but the last time he'd talked about books, Freddy had called him a loser.

Danny knew he wasn't a loser. There was nothing wrong with reading books. But for some reason, Freddy and Teddy only liked him when Mrs. Contreras came to visit.

"Do you have your permission slip?" Mrs. Garner asked them.

The twins groaned and Danny nodded while stuffing his mouth full of pancakes before Freddy could take them from his plate.

"Where are they taking you again?" Mr. Garner asked. His thick gray eyebrows were knit close together like two caterpillars kissing.

"The *library*," Teddy groaned. Danny could tell the twins apart easily now because Teddy had lost a tooth after fighting with another kid last month.

"What's so great about this library?" Mr. Garner asked, not taking his eyes off his paper. He licked his thumb and turned the page.

"It's the one in Manhattan," Danny said. "The big one with the lions out front and special rooms."

"I don't see what's so special there that you can't find at a library here in Staten Island," his foster father said.

Danny kept quiet. He knew not to contradict him or ever say anything disparaging about Staten Island. Besides, Danny wasn't sure if Mr. Garner had ever stepped foot inside a library, so how would he know?

"Can I stay home, Pop?" Freddy asked.

"Yeah, Pop," Teddy said. "It's Friday. We can start the weekend early and throw the ball around."

Freddy rolled his bright blue eyes to the back of his head. Teddy copied his every move. They had the same dusty-blond hair and mean pink pout. "Not Danny, though. He can't even throw a ball."

"I'm sure Danny can throw a ball," Mrs. Garner said. Her voice was quiet, like a mouse trying to shout behind a plaster wall. She sat down to eat the last two pancakes and a single leftover slice of bacon.

Teddy reached out with his thick hand and grabbed the bacon. In one second, he shoved it into his mouth without saying please or thank you.

"What are *you* looking at?" Freddy asked Danny.

Danny tried not to jump as he felt a terrible pinch on his leg. If he looked under the table, he knew he'd see Freddy pinching him. Danny felt angry and kicked out without thinking.

"Pop!" Freddy shouted. He made a whimpering sound and held his leg with a dramatic flair, as if Danny had wounded him mortally. "Danny kicked me!"

"He pinched me first!" Danny shouted, but one look at Mr. Garner's face and Danny knew it was a lost cause. His foster father never believed him.

Mr. Garner slammed his fist on the table. "What did I tell you about disrespecting my boys?"

"But—"

"No *buts*." Mr. Garner kept talking. Freddy and Teddy smirked at Danny, taking pleasure in Danny's misfortune. Mrs. Garner looked down at her plate and ate her pancakes. He wanted her to wake up. He wanted her to stand up for him, because in the whole house, she was the kindest one. The one who sewed patches on his holey backpack and the ripped seams on his shirts. "What did I tell you?"

"Henry," Mrs. Garner said. But it was so quiet that Danny wasn't sure if he'd imagined it or not.

"Well?" Mr. Garner asked.

Freddy and Teddy held their hands over their mouths to stop from giggling. Maybe they hadn't pranked him first thing in the morning like most days. But they knew they'd get him in trouble eventually.

"If I so much as look at Freddy and Teddy the wrong way," Danny said, like he was reciting from a script he knew all too well, "I'm going right back to the group home I came from."

"Is that what you want?" Mr. Garner asked.

Danny pressed his lips together.

He set his fork on the table. He wasn't hungry anymore. He leveled his eyes with Mr. Garner. They were a mean shade of blue, like dark waters. Danny imagined if Mr. Garner were in a storybook, he'd be a terribly rude pirate. Except that pirates were cool sometimes. An ogre was more like it. Danny didn't want to cry in front of Mr. Garner, but he felt his lip tremble, so he kept quiet and thought of the one person who made him feel brave: Pili. Long gone, run-away Pili.

Mr. Garner sighed. He ran his fingers through his thinning hair and sank into his chair. "I don't want to be the bad guy, Danny. But you can't keep behaving this way. You're lucky we took you in."

Danny knew he wasn't the lucky one. He knew the reason the Garners kept him around, and it wasn't because they wanted to make their family bigger. He'd heard Mr. Garner talking about the check he'd get for Danny. The thing was, that money should have been used for Danny's care and clothes and food. Instead, it seemed to go to the bills piling up on the rickety table at the door entrance.

"I'm sorry," Danny said to the twins, even though he knew he'd done nothing wrong. One day, he'd be far away, and Freddy and Teddy would wish they'd been nicer to him.

In a matter of seconds, Mr. Garner went back to his sports section and Mrs. Garner started cleaning up and Freddy and Teddy started fighting over the last Pop-Tart in the box. Danny washed his plate and set it on the drying rack. It was the least he could do to help Mrs. Garner. Then the bus beeped outside their house and, as usual, Danny was the first one out of the house.

He hopped onto the bus and handed Ms. Esposito his permission slip. Everyone usually called her Ms. Explosito because she always looked like something had exploded around her. Her short, light brown hair stood on end and her makeup was always smudged around her eyes from rubbing them when she was nervous or forgetful or stressed (which was always).

"Good morning, Ms. Esposito," Danny said, and took his seat in the front row. No one likes the front-row seat of the bus, but it was better than sitting anywhere near the twins and their friends, who liked to take turns putting gum in Danny's hair or putting things down the back of his shirt.

The twins ignored Danny as they took their seats somewhere in the back. Unless they were using him as target practice, they didn't want to be associated with their foster brother, and that was all right with Danny.

The bus doors hissed closed. As he settled in, he noticed a shadow stretched on the ceiling. For one moment, it seemed to detach itself and take the shape of a person. Danny froze. The last time he'd seen something like that was with Mrs. Haydenson at the library. His imagination, his belief, had gotten him in so much trouble. It had to stop. Danny shut his eyes and counted backward from ten. He repeated the words he'd learned with Mrs. Contreras. *There are no moving shadows. There is no such thing as magic.* He was so full of missing Pili, he was imagining something that wasn't there.

When he opened his eyes, the shadows were still. Ordinary. Just like him. Danny clutched his backpack and stared out the bus window all the way to Manhattan.

←6→
The Way to New York City

THE YELLOW BUS PULLED up right in front of the New York Public Library. It was the grandest, most magnificent building Danny had ever seen. There was nothing like it on Staten Island.

Ms. Esposito let everyone out and they gathered in front of the bus. *Hundreds* of people walked on the street around them. Tourists took pictures in front of the great big lion statues and on the steps. There was a green lawn right next to the library called Bryant Park, where people were spread across the grass, or clustered around metal tables and chairs. Other kids his age seemed to be on a similar field trip, and they lined up through the front door. Danny craned his neck, but the buildings just kept reaching toward the sky. The air smelled like car exhaust but also food from nearby hot dog and pretzel vendors. He could even smell popcorn wafting on the breeze from the theaters in Times Square a few blocks away.

Mr. Garner always talked about how much he hated Manhattan, but Danny buzzed with excitement. Nothing, not even Freddy and Teddy moaning and groaning as they filed off the bus, could put a damper on today.

As they ascended the library steps, Freddy had his eyes narrowed in Danny's direction. Freddy smirked in a way that told Danny the twins were up to no good. Last time they had schemed like that, they covered his seat with clear glue and Danny got stuck to his chair. Danny hoped being out in public would make the twins behave, but he wasn't going to hold his breath. He followed Ms. Esposito.

This library was unlike any he'd ever seen. The surfaces were a tan, polished stone. In the lobby, two giant archways created a doorway to what looked like the library stacks Danny was used to. He craned his neck back to get a good look at the chandeliers and intricately carved ceilings. Danny thought that this was what a palace might look like. Though he'd never been to a palace in his life.

They were met at the entrance by a young librarian with blue hair and a dress covered in lemons. She had deep brown skin and a diamond piercing on her nose.

"I'm Anjali Singh and I'm your tour guide for the day," she said as they gathered in a corner. "Today I'll be taking you into some of our special rooms, like the latest rare-book room and our collection of city maps. Before we get started, do you have any questions?"

"What makes a book rare?" Kelly Park asked. She had shiny black hair and kind black eyes that crinkled at the corners when she smiled, and she smiled a lot.

Anjali grinned and her nose ring caught the light. "Excellent question. Things that are rare are hard to find. They're one of a kind, unique, and oftentimes irreplaceable. We've had texts found in desert caves, abandoned author homes. Our latest acquisition was found in Central Park, but that one is still being restored."

Danny started to consider what a strange place a park would be to find an irreplaceable book, but his eyes kept finding different things to be distracted by. He'd never seen so many people in a library before. Tourists were taking photos in front of plaques and the large doors. People looked like they had traveled from all over the world to be here. That filled Danny with a sense of wonder. Usually the twins made fun of him for liking the library, but in that moment, he didn't feel so strange and out of place for loving books. Speaking of his foster brothers, Freddy and Teddy and their friends were taking turns testing their echoes, which bounced in the long stairwells.

"Follow me and stay together," the tour guide said, and led them toward the special rooms and exhibits on the second floor.

As they climbed the stairs, Danny caught sight of a girl about his age, zigzagging her way through the lobby. She carried a stack of books up to her chin. The books looked like they might topple over at any second, but she somehow balanced them all as she went through one of the archways and out of sight.

The hair on the back of Danny's neck prickled. He grabbed hold of the railing and glanced around. His mind went straight for the memory of the moving shadows on the bus. He searched for another explanation. The library was ancient and probably had lots of drafty corridors. He'd left his sweater on the bus.

Just then, Danny felt a force against his shoulders. The air left his lungs as he flew forward. He caught himself right before he fell on the floor.

"Watch your step!" Teddy shouted behind him.

Danny felt his face turn bright red with anger as he dusted his hands and stood back up. He forced himself to take a deep breath as the twins ran to catch up to the rest of the class. His teacher and the tour guide hadn't noticed, but there was a ring of titters and pitying glances from his classmates. He didn't want to let them spoil this day, but he couldn't help it. Danny's blood boiled, and he couldn't force his feet to follow the others.

At the top of the stairs, he went the opposite direction.

He knew the rules. Do not separate from your group. Do not wander on your own. Do not get lost. But wasn't that what he was? A lost boy.

Danny's heavy feet echoed down the long hallway of smooth marble floors. This place was so fancy there were gold flecks on the ground. He pretended he was in some great home that belonged to him alone. Ahead of him was a corridor of closed doors. Were all these rooms full of rare books like the tour guide said? In that moment, he wished more than *anything* that Pili were with him. She'd make up a story to go with every door and turn it magical. A room filled with never-ending kettle corn. A room where it was always summer outside. A room that always had the book you were looking for . . . Two years and three months had passed without seeing her and he missed her more than ever. But thinking of her this way made his gloom fade.

Bright sunlight filled the hallway from an intricate metal window at the end. Danny wasn't ready to return to his class yet. He turned the door handles and peered into empty rooms along the way. One looked like an old-fashioned classroom. Another was filled to the brim with dusty, old books and a table full of unopened mail. He didn't think he should be there, so he closed the door.

As he let his anger drain from his body, Danny slowed his pace. Each of his footsteps made an echo, and for a moment he was afraid that he'd get in big trouble for leaving the group. But no one had come looking for him. Sometimes it made Danny angry how invisible he felt. Other times, like now, it was freeing.

The warm, early September sun shone down on him.

From this side of the building it was like everything, from the walls to the floors and everything in between, was painted in gold. Danny remembered a story Pili would tell him, about a lost city of gold.

"I wish you were here, Pili," he said out loud. But his voice was too small and low in the great wide corridor.

Danny began to turn and follow the sound of Anjali's voice, but a flash of movement caught his eye. He whirled around and expected to see Freddy and Teddy playing games with him.

The only footsteps on the marble were his own. The only shadow on the ground was his. But the sound he heard was not coming from the lobby full of tourists. It surrounded him. At first, it was like listening to wind chimes blowing in the breeze. The metallic clinks moved all around him, louder and louder. Danny tried to cover his ears but it didn't muffle the sound. The prickling sensation on the back of his neck returned and he didn't have the twins to explain it.

That was when he realized that the golden light wasn't coming from the windows but from beneath his feet. For a moment, Danny couldn't believe what he was seeing. He took several steps back and rubbed his eyes like he did when he woke up after a dream.

The floor lit up with golden ribbons and vines. At first, he thought that there were strips of light in the ground. But what was appearing beneath his very feet was incandescent and pure gold. There was only one word he would use: *magic*. There were dozens of them, shaped like curling arrows and twisting roots. Danny was struck with a sense of familiarity. But he'd never seen anything as marvelous as this. Some golden lines swirled in rings, like puppies who chased their own tails. Others wiggled like garden snakes between blades of grass. Light flooded the hall, like it was right beneath the tiles, waiting to burst out. He crouched down and tried to touch one golden arrow, but it only felt cold, like sticking a finger in a glass of ice water.

Danny closed his eyes. He counted backward from ten. *There is no such thing as magic.* He repeated the words in his mind, then out loud. But these weren't shadows. This was something else entirely.

He looked again. He could feel his heart racing as he opened his left eye and then his right.

The arrows were still there. Their gold light lit up on the surface of the marble tiles. Danny took a step, and they moved forward, the sharp points turning in one direction.

"This *can't* be real," Danny said. Who was he trying to convince? Himself or the grown-ups in his life?

A small voice in his mind whispered, *Of course it's real.*

Danny glanced over his shoulder. No one had noticed he was gone yet. He lifted his feet and tested to see what would happen if he walked away. The arrows froze. He set his foot back on the tile. The arrows whirled and pointed in the opposite direction of where he was walking. They wanted Danny to turn around.

"Where are you taking me?" Danny whispered. He cut a glance down the hall, but the coast was clear. He wasn't sure how he'd explain this, or even if he could.

His mind was a carousel of thoughts. First, he knew he was breaking the promise he'd made Mrs. Contreras. But the golden arrows had appeared to Danny. He hadn't gone looking for them. The arrows undulated again, and with every step he took, they led the way to the dead end of the hall. Danny sucked in a breath as the arrows disappeared from beneath him. They'd moved whippet fast ahead.

"Slow down!" Danny whisper-shouted, though he wasn't sure if the golden arrows could understand.

He hurried along, following the swirling, illuminated lines until they climbed up the last door in the corridor.

Danny looked down the hall. He already wasn't supposed to be there, he most *definitely* shouldn't be opening a closed door, and he *most, most definitely* shouldn't be talking to magical glowing arrows. He could just picture the disappointment on Mrs. Contreras's face when he tried to explain it to her. Worst of all, the anger on Mr. Garner's face if they got a call about Danny breaking into rooms he shouldn't be going into.

But what about what Danny wanted? He realized he'd also given up on his promise to his sister. *Remember.* He had to remember magic, fairy tales, wishes, stars. He had to remember that Pili was out there somewhere.

The vines grew brighter and brighter. Their light made him squint as they wrapped themselves around the brass handle and their force swung the door open.

The lights were off, but rays of sunshine broke through the windows and illuminated the bare room. Unlike the cluttered spaces he'd peeked into up the hall, this room had only a long table encased in glass. There were no paintings, no shelves, no plaques on the walls. It was like the only thing that mattered was whatever was displayed in that table at the center of the room. Danny took a step and the wooden floorboards made a sound that reminded him of his eighty-year-old neighbor moaning about her joints. As he approached, the gold arrows slid from the ground and up over the table. They sort of looked like the ivy that clung to the side of a really old building in his neighborhood.

Danny stepped closer, one careful foot at a time.

There, under the glass, was a book laid open. It seemed small, considering it had an entire table for itself. The pages were faded and splotchy, like paper dipped in brown tea and left out to dry. One time Ms. Esposito made them do that for an art project, but these pages were truly old. Fine slanted letters were scribbled in black ink. He thought of what the tour guide had said about rare books. This one was so special it had an entire room to itself! Danny wished he could open the glass to have a better look, but he was afraid of setting off any alarms. He glanced up, but there didn't seem to be any cameras in the high ceilings. He *had* seen *Mission: Impossible* because of Mr. Garner, so he knew he should at least *look*.

Danny stopped inches from the enclosed glass. The gold arrows were now traveling along the clear surface and seeping into the open book, like invisible ink. What kind of book *was* this? He peered around for a small placard or sign, the way they usually had at museums. But there was nothing.

Upon closer inspection, Danny noted that it was a hard-back, the kind with a cloth cover. The book was open down the middle, written in precise, neat handwriting. The glow of gold warmed Danny's face as the light that had seeped into the book shone from within the slanted script letters. It was as if a sunbeam was passing across the page and illuminating the words beneath.

Just as quickly as they had appeared, the golden arrows and vines vanished. Danny pressed his hands on the surface, leaving behind smudgy fingerprints.

"No! Come back!"

The unmistakable sound of a dog barking made Danny jump. The growl echoed in the room. He wasn't alone anymore. He hadn't even heard anyone come in.

"You're not supposed to be here," a sharp voice scolded him.

Danny whirled around and shrank back, accidentally rattling the glass case behind him. The dog snarled and lowered itself onto its front paws the way animals did when they were going to jump, or worse, bite.

"I'm sorry," Danny said. His voice came out in a whoosh of air. "The door was open. Well, it opened on its own, really."

The girl in front of him had freckled, light brown skin;

inquisitive brown eyes; and a pert, round nose. She wore a bright yellow dress, and her brown curls were swept up into two buns atop her head. He recognized her as the same girl he'd seen carrying a stack of books nearly as tall as she was. Only now she didn't have any books. Her hands were at her hips and her eyes were narrowed to slits as she stared at him. She seemed no older than Danny himself. Her shoes were Mary Janes the color of candied apples and her white socks were pulled right up to her knees.

"What do you mean it opened on its own?" the girl asked warily.

Danny was torn between lying and telling the truth. He knew she wouldn't believe him. No one did. But he was going to get in trouble either way, so he might as well be honest.

"I saw something," Danny explained. "I can't explain *what* I saw, but the door opened on its own, I swear. Now, will you please stop your dog from trying to eat me?"

She rolled her eyes. "He's not going to *eat you*. Orion, be nice."

Orion, a small Pomeranian, sat up and made a whining sound. If Danny could speak the same language as dogs, he imagined it would be translated into *What did* I *do?*

"Thanks," Danny said, easing a bit.

"Don't thank me yet," she said, eyeing him with a curious spark. "Who are you?"

"I'm Danny. I got separated from my school tour." Danny turned to point at the glass case. "What is this book?"

The girl's face lit up and she closed the distance between them. It was as if he'd finally asked the right question. "Isn't it cool? This is the original book of fairy tales written by Ella St. Clay. It's called *The Way to Rio Luna*."

←7→
The Boy and the Lucky Squirrel

IF DANNY HAD BEEN holding something, he would have dropped it dramatically. Instead, he stood there, his mouth open so wide he could probably double as a fly catcher.

He stared at the book with reverence, and as his eyes traced the handwritten letters, he realized it was his favorite story: "Sinchi and the Cliffs of Nowhere."

"I know this one," Danny said, feeling a bit dazed as his throat tightened with emotion. It was his book. Pili's book. At least, it was a version of it. He never thought he'd see it again and it was here, in this library, bathed in the same golden light that had beckoned him.

"You do?" the girl asked. Her eyes widened with excitement. "There were only a thousand copies printed and then the publisher burned down. My auntie tells me that's why they're so special."

"Rare," Danny said, remembering what Anjali the tour guide had told them.

"Exactly. Do you still have your copy?"

Danny shook his head. "No. But my sister used to read this book of stories to me. Her favorite one was about the Moon Witch."

"I love that one!" the girl in the yellow dress said. "My mom also read it to me when I was little."

They grinned at each other. It had been so long since he'd met someone he shared something in common with. Could this curious girl see the golden arrows, too?

"Wait, why is it locked up?" Danny asked her.

"For security reasons, mostly." The girl shrugged. "An archeologist working for the library is trying to restore it."

"That must be the book Ms. Singh mentioned."

"Yes. My auntie is the one doing the restoration."

Danny leaned back over the glass pane. The book was old, but it looked in better condition than the copy he'd owned.

"What does that mean? What's wrong with it?" he asked.

"Four pages are missing and the ink has some water damage." She drummed her fingers on the glass display. "Can you believe it? Ella St. Clay's real handwriting. It's nothing like my handwriting, which is messy. But I'm working on my calligraphy. Anyway, one thing is for sure. It's a special book."

Danny agreed wholeheartedly. It was special. Could the girl in the yellow dress tell him more? Was there a chance he wasn't the only one who could see the gold arrows? Would she make fun of him for asking? He needed to know, so he worked up the courage to ask.

"What about— I mean— Can you see the arrows, too?" he asked tentatively, wincing like he was getting ready for the slap of words that confirmed he was just as strange as grown-ups had told him his whole life.

"Arrows?" A tiny wrinkle formed across her brow. She seemed to take a step closer to him. He imagined if she had a magnifying glass, she'd peer at him through it.

"They're the ones who opened the door—" He was beginning to worry that he'd said something wrong and was about to backtrack when a golden arrow materialized on the open pages of the original Ella St. Clay book. It darted across the page, then went right through the glass. It vanished in a puff of glitter right at Danny's feet.

Both Danny and the girl gasped.

"There! Did you see that?" Danny said.

"Wait right here." She pointed a finger in his face. Orion started barking again.

"Where are you going?" Danny shouted, but she was already running out the door and down the corridor.

Danny shook. What if she was getting security? What if the arrows meant something terrible? He couldn't get in trouble again. The more the moments dragged, the more Danny convinced himself that this girl was going to tell on him. She was going to say a strange boy had broken into a room with a rare book and started rambling on about golden arrows. Then he'd have to face Mr. Garner and Ms. Esposito and Mrs. Contreras and Anjali. Why couldn't he have ignored the arrows? Why had he let the twins drive him away in the first place? He couldn't be here if she returned with security guards.

Danny ran out the door, slamming it shut. With every step, frantic golden arrows appeared beneath his feet, bending into U-turns on the floor. They wanted him to go back.

"No! You can't follow me," Danny told the arrows. Great. Now he was talking to them. Mrs. Contreras would not like that.

His sneakers made screeching sounds as he skidded down the hall. A bright lemon-printed fabric caught his eyes, and he barreled up the flight of stairs, nearly bumping into the tour guide, Anjali Singh. To his relief, the golden arrows beneath his feet faded. Was it because he'd gone too far from the room with Ella St. Clay's book?

"Hello there!" the librarian said in her friendly, high-pitched voice.

"Hi, sorry, I took a wrong turn," Danny said, trying to catch his breath. He nearly doubled over at the top of the stairs. He could hear the girl and the dog barking down below. Who was she? Dogs weren't allowed in the library.

"That's all right," Anjali said, smiling with white teeth and sparkly nose ring. "Your class is right down the hall. I forgot my notes. Is everything okay?"

Danny's mouth was dry from running, so he nodded rapidly. Though he didn't feel completely okay. Perhaps he *hadn't* imagined the moving shadow on the bus that morning. But that shadow had been different from the golden arrows. The shadow was a prickly sensation. The arrows were warm.

When Danny and Anjali stepped into a wide room full of maps, he sighed with relief. No security was coming for him. His classmates were crowded in front of posters depicting what Manhattan looked like a hundred years ago. Ms. Esposito was drumming her fingers on a small wooden table, checking her phone. The twins were whispering in a corner. Had no one truly noticed that he'd been gone?

Was he so invisible?

Then another sensation gripped him. It settled right between his ribs. It was like losing something you loved all over again. He knew that he couldn't have taken the book. It was protected beneath glass. But after so much time separated from Ella St. Clay's book, he'd been so close to touching it. To reading the stories after feeling like he was forgetting the words.

The librarian pointed to a map secured beneath the glass as she spoke about the tunnels beneath the city, and the blueprints for Central Park. When she started talking about abandoned forts with old passageways, Teddy and Freddy threw their heads back and made snoring noises. Ms. Esposito rubbed her eyes and tried her best to silence the roar of laughter from the class.

"No flash!" a security guard shouted, and stomped into the room.

Kelly Park had been trying to take a picture of the maps with her cell phone. She shrugged and shoved the phone into her pocket. They spent the rest of the morning exploring the lower levels of the library, and by the time they broke for lunch, Danny saw no signs of the golden arrows or the mysterious girl and her dog. He was starting to think he'd imagined them, too. He should have been relieved. He could go about his day and be the kind of boy Mrs. Contreras wanted him to be: good and ordinary. The kind of boy who didn't see shadows moving on their own or follow golden arrows into locked rooms.

On the way out, Kelly and her friends clogged up the doorway trying to take a selfie. They winked and stuck out their tongues. Kelly's arms were covered in temporary tattoos that her parents allowed her to have. She smiled at Danny and waved him over.

"Me?" he asked, and glanced back over his shoulder. No one was there, so surely it had to be him.

"Yeah! Group selfie time."

Danny had never been asked to be part of a group before.

Not unless it was forced on them by a class activity. It was hard to make friends when he'd moved so often, and Teddy and Freddy were always there to tell people how *uncool* and *weird* Danny was. Could Kelly Park be a friend he could talk to? He wished there was *someone* he could tell about the peculiar things he'd seen that day. Maybe this group selfie was the start of a new friendship. But as he began walking over to them, Teddy barreled into him.

Danny managed not to topple over, but by the time he'd steadied himself, Freddy and Teddy had replaced him in Kelly's group.

"Come on, kids," Ms. Esposito said, and ushered everyone out.

Danny lingered in the map room as long as he could. He was embarrassed about Teddy pushing him, but mostly he was sad. He'd seen something extraordinary and there was no one to share it with. It was the kind of sadness that made him want to curl into a ball and fall asleep until the bad day had passed. When was the last time he'd felt excited?

It was when he'd made plans with Pili. The days when he'd convinced himself that he had found magic. That moment when he saw the golden arrows and when he talked to the girl in the yellow dress. He wanted that feeling back. Right now, he needed a miracle.

———————

As they spilled a few yards into Bryant Park for lunch, Anjali shouted, "Don't forget to sign up for your library cards!" Danny and his class ate beside the library on the bright green lawn. He unzipped his backpack and took out his hand sanitizer. After living with the twins, Danny carried it everywhere he went because Teddy and Freddy liked to leave their boogers all over the place.

He sat by himself and opened the brown paper bag lunch that the school provided.

"Hey, Danoodle," Teddy said, marching up to where he was. "Give me your cookie."

Danny looked up at him. The other kids were looking at them. Ms. Esposito was all the way across the lawn, chatting with the tour guide. Even if she was there, she never seemed to see the moments that the twins chose to torture him.

"Why are you so mean to him?" Kelly Park asked. She pursed her lips and crossed her arms over her chest. "Isn't he your brother?"

"No, he isn't! Mind your business," Teddy shouted at her.

Danny tried to give Kelly a small smile, but all his insides felt like they were being liquefied in a blender. It was supposed to be a good day. He was in a place he'd always dreamed of visiting. He'd seen Ella St. Clay's handwritten book of the stories he loved. He'd made a new friend. Sort of. But the twins were never going to let him have any kind of happiness. Anger filled Danny's heart. He didn't *want* to be their brother, either, but he didn't have a choice. He stood up and faced Teddy. It was unusual that he'd be without his twin.

"I said, give me your cookie," Teddy said.

"No."

"What did you say to me?"

Danny felt his feet grow heavy, as if he were sinking into cement. "I said, no, you can't have my cookie."

Then came a cackling laugh from behind him. Danny turned to find Freddy holding both of Danny's candy bars. He'd stolen them right out of his backpack. Danny was so angry he was shaking.

As the boys ran off with the thieved chocolate, Danny zipped his backpack shut again and ate his lunch in silence while the other kids sat in groups. Kelly gave him a small smile and waved him over, but he didn't want to be any-where near the Garner twins.

A squirrel approached him carefully. It was thin and small, with a fluffy long tail. Danny held a piece of bread out to it. "Here you go, buddy."

He could swear the squirrel winked at him. It was a day of impossibilities, so why was this any different?

While his class filed into the gift shop, Danny dragged his feet behind the chaperone onto the bus. He sat in the front-row seat all by himself.

He thought about what a strange day it had been. He wondered what his sister would have done if she was in his shoes. Pili wouldn't have gotten scared. When the girl in yellow ran off, Pili would have waited, no matter what the outcome. She also would have kept following the arrows to see what they could possibly want. Pili was braver than he had ever felt. Mrs. Contreras once told him that the pain of being without his sister would get easier. But that wasn't true.

"I wish you were here," he said out loud.

"What was that, kid?" the bus driver asked.

"Oh, nothing, just singing out loud," Danny said, his

cheeks growing warm with embarrassment. The last thing he needed was an adult to think he was talking to himself. He had pulled his backpack onto his lap when he realized it wasn't zipped all the way. Before he could close it, a burst of gold escaped from inside. Startled, he dropped the bag. He glanced around, but none of the other kids filing in had noticed anything. Danny's heart hammered, and he reached for his pack again. There was another burst of gold, like the sparkler candles the twins had for their birthday two weeks ago. It popped, like it was trying to get his attention, then vanished.

Danny reached into his bag.

There was something there that shouldn't have been.

A worn old hardcover book. He hadn't checked anything out of the library and the only person who had gone through his bag was one of the twins. Had the twins done this to get him in trouble? Danny glanced around the bus, a sinking feeling in his chest. He pulled the book out and held it with trembling hands.

The book jacket was wrapped in dark blue cloth with embroidered gold leaves twisting like vines and a giant bright eight-pointed star at the center. He turned it in his hands, the palms of his skin buzzing with a numb sensation, like he'd fallen asleep with his arm over his head. He shook a hand to make the feeling go away, then traced the letters on the spine with his index finger. *The Way to Rio Luna* by Ella St. Clay.

"No way," Danny exhaled. His mouth was dry and he blinked several times to make sure he was seeing things right. His whole body felt lit up from the inside, like there were cherry bombs in his heart. He repeated, "No way."

Yes way, said a little voice in the back of his head. The voice that sounded like Pili giving him advice.

Danny thumbed through the pages. Each handwritten story had a small illustration at the top. The paper was thick, unlike most books. The ink had faded in some sections, but he recognized the stories. "The Moon Witch in the Red Woods," "Sinchi and the Cliffs of Nowhere," and another one about giants and a runaway king. It felt like seeing old friends.

The book was real and solid.

And then it occurred to him . . . he most definitely shouldn't have it. How had it gotten in his backpack from the glass casing?

More of his classmates boarded the bus, laughing and showing one another trinkets from the store. No one looked his way or at what he was holding. Just in case, Danny shoved the book back in his pack and worried at his lip. What should he do? If he confessed to having the book, he might get in trouble for stealing. If he took it, he would *actually* be stealing. Could Freddy and Teddy have done it to mess with him again? Once, they took their father's signed Derek Jeter baseball and hid it under Danny's pillow. Danny thought Mr. Garner would shake the house apart with all his screaming.

But how could the twins have gotten their hands on the book to begin with? It had been well protected. If not them, then who?

The golden light. Danny was sure of it. But who would believe that golden sparks brought the book to him? It couldn't be a coincidence that the arrows showed him the way to the locked room, and then sparks of the same color appeared in his pack. There was something at work that he couldn't explain yet, but he needed answers. He wasn't going to get them on this bus.

As everyone took their seats, Danny knew what he had to do. He took the book out of his backpack and clutched it against his chest. Ms. Esposito was crossing everyone's names off her attendance list.

"Ms. Esposito," he said. His whole mouth was as dry as

Mrs. Garner's meat loaf. He breathed hard and fast. He didn't want to get in trouble, but he couldn't take the book home, even if it meant looking like a thief.

"Yes, Danny?" she said. "Ashley, sit down! Gaby, raise your hand. Put that down right now!"

As he held the book, he gave it one last look. He wished he could keep it. But it wouldn't be right. When he thumbed through the pages, something fell from the back and fluttered to the ground at his feet.

He bent down to pick up it up. It was the library checkout card. Danny stared at the names. Even those were written in gold! There were dates stamped in different colors and fonts, but one specific name leapt out at him. It was a name he would know anywhere. A name he'd said thousands of times. For a moment, his vision was blurred, like looking out the window while it was raining. Danny pressed the checkout card to his chest, right over his heart. The name there was clear and real and he had not imagined it. *Pili Monteverde* was written in round letters. The date was marked today exactly two years ago, after his sister was believed to have run away.

He took a deep breath and wiped at his cheeks. He started to sit but his teacher finally noticed him.

"Danny, what is it?" Ms. Esposito asked hurriedly.

He felt a jolt of panic. Danny couldn't *leave* now. For the first time, he had proof that Pili was out there. She'd written her name on the card herself. Did she truly run away or was she hiding somewhere? He thought of the times he'd seen her in his dreams or the moments when he thought he caught sight of her at the corner of his eye. Could those moments have been messages? Was that why the arrows had guided him?

He had to go back inside the library. Perhaps the girl in the sun-yellow dress could help. She knew where this book had been found. If Pili was the last person to have checked it out, then *maybe*, just maybe, there was some information that could lead Danny to her. He knew that he could not stay on that bus. He couldn't go back to the Garners. He wished he had a distraction.

"Well?" Ms. Esposito asked, but she wasn't looking at him. "We have to leave now or we'll be stuck on the bridge for hours."

And his wish was answered when a scream came from the back of the bus.

"Get it off me!" Teddy shouted.

Everyone screamed except for Danny. A thin gray

squirrel had gripped Teddy's head and was scratching him. Ms. Esposito dropped her clipboard on her seat, and everyone moved toward the back to save Teddy, even the bus driver.

At any other moment, this sight would've filled Danny with glee. But right now he couldn't focus on anything except the rectangular card with his sister's name on it. He closed his eyes and counted backward from ten, out of habit. Mrs. Contreras had tried to convince him that magic wasn't real, but today proved that Danny was onto something. The moving shadows, the dream, the golden arrows. Even the girl in the yellow dress and her dog. Now this book. Magic was around him, and he couldn't doubt himself again.

"Magic is real," he said instead.

When he looked, Pili's name was still written there.

He knew he had to go. Perhaps no family would ever want to take him in again. But Danny didn't care. Without Pili, he'd always be an orphan, lost and alone and invisible. She had written her name in this book two years ago. She was somewhere out there now. Adults weren't good at listening to him, so he had to find another way to help.

Danny draped his sweater on the back of his seat, zipped

up his backpack, and while everyone was paying attention to Teddy and the squirrel, Danny hopped off the bus and raced up the library steps.

When he reached the top of the steps, he turned to look back. The thin squirrel hopped out of the doors just as they shut. The bus was leaving without him.

There was no turning back now. Danny's heart beat like a kick drum in his chest because he was on his own, he was breaking the rules, and he would do whatever it took to find his sister.

The Girl Made of Colors

DANNY WAS MANY THINGS. He was a chameleon who could fade into the background. He was a good student. He was an orphan. And now he was a runaway.

For what seemed like the longest minute of his life, Danny watched the school bus drive away. How long would it take before anyone noticed that he wasn't in his seat? Would they turn right around? Or would they get all the way back to Staten Island before Ms. Esposito looked over to see that Danny wasn't there?

A terrible feeling filled his chest as he imagined what might happen to him. Where was he going to sleep? He'd never taken public transportation on his own and he didn't have enough money to buy more than one meal. But he'd have to handle that later. After a whole two years he finally had proof that Pili was somewhere. She had held this very book and written her name down in the card.

Danny pulled open the heavy library door and stepped back inside, holding the clothbound book tightly in his arms. He'd never owned anything that cost much. His clothes were all hand-me-downs, and the times he'd been given gifts for Christmas or his birthday, they had usually been shoes and socks and underwear. For the first time, he understood what the word *priceless* meant. *Rare.*

The lobby of the New York Public Library was the same as it had been earlier that morning. Tourists still took pictures next to stone pillars and on the ancient-looking steps. A bald man with olive-toned skin carried a tote bag full of books past him. The tote bag read I HATE TOTE BAGS.

Danny chuckled to himself and took a moment to figure out his next move. For the moment, he was safe. Even though he'd done a reckless thing, part of him felt free. He was away from the Garners. Away from everything he knew. He should feel more afraid, but the promise of finding out more about this book fueled him. All he needed now was someone to believe his story. Believe in him.

He took a final steadying breath and walked past a group of women in flowery skirts and several college-aged kids who looked like they hadn't slept in days. The library smelled like air conditioner and that strange smell old paper has. The lights were fluorescent and had a white tinge that made him feel exposed. He stopped in front of one of the librarians at the nearest counter. He cleared his throat but she didn't look up at anyone who walked by, not even Danny, who was right in front of her. No one had noticed him all day except for the girl in the yellow dress. He regretted not having waited for her. He wished he'd gotten her name. Then it occurred to him. He could ask for Anjali! The librarian with the lemon-printed dress. She had known all about rare books. Sometimes it helped to retrace your steps in order to remember things. The last time he'd seen her she'd been on the second floor.

He walked slowly toward the stairs and noticed a large group of security guards. Danny heard the static of a walkie-talkie.

"Code . . . in the building . . ." a voice came through the

walkie-talkie interspersed with static. Though he couldn't understand everything through the bad connection, the person on the other end of the radio sounded urgent. He'd watched enough cop shows to know that "codes" stood for something. What if the code was about the missing book? What if they arrested him before he had a chance to explain? Danny couldn't tell them that he'd run away from his field trip, that he'd been left behind and he had a mysterious book that he had *definitely* not stolen from the display case. Worst of all, he couldn't admit to seeing things. If there was one thing he was sure of, it was that adults did not like it when kids told the truth, because it always sounded like a made-up story.

He was beginning to think that he'd made a series of very grave mistakes. As the security guards spread out, carefully watching the library patrons, Danny made his way to the stairs. He kept his eyes on the ground and, though he tried to remain calm, his heart felt like a brick in his throat as he ascended the steps.

The halls were empty. His sneakers made squeaky noises the faster he walked. He stuck his head in the map room, but there was only a family of four taking pictures. *With* flash. The security guard from earlier didn't seem to be around. He looked into two more rooms, but there was no sign of Anjali.

He went back down the other corridor to the room where the book had been on display. With each step, he hoped the golden arrows would appear, but when he reached the end of the hall, there was nothing but ordinary marble floors. He jostled the doorknob but it was locked.

"Oh no," Danny said breathlessly. He held the book at eye level. Magic was unpredictable, he knew that from the stories he'd read. "Now would be a good time to open the door again."

The slightest hope the book might somehow be a wishing genie vanished. He heard the static of security guards in the distance. He was going to be caught red-handed. All the warnings that Mrs. Contreras had given him piled up in his mind. Be good. Behave. Don't do anything crazy. How he *hated* that word, *crazy*. It was only used by people who didn't believe him.

He couldn't give up yet. He couldn't leave the library without finding out why his sister had checked out this book. Even if it meant hiding from security. He marched back up the hall and tried each doorknob. They were all locked!

"Come on," Danny muttered. His belly felt like there

were worms twisting themselves into knots. He heard heavy boot steps coming upstairs.

He tried one more door. It was one of the rooms he'd accidentally stumbled into earlier. The walls were crowded with old books. Curtains were held open by fringed cords. Two wooden tables were stacked with letters, papers, pens, magnifying glasses. One desk had an old-fashioned-looking phone, the kind he'd only ever seen in movies, and lamps with thick green glass. This room smelled old. One librarian had once told him that the smell of books actually came from moldy paper. He didn't care if it was book mold or not. That scent always made him think of Pili.

Then he realized he wasn't alone.

Standing in the corner, holding a scroll of paper, was the girl in the yellow dress!

"It's you!" he said.

She froze at the sight of him, her big brown eyes crinkled at the corners. "Of course it's me! Where did you go?"

In all his life, he'd never seen a girl wear so many bright colors all at once. It felt like every time he looked at her, he noticed something new. A plastic blue watch on her wrist. Dozens of rainbow jelly bracelets on her right arm. A small metallic book pin on the top of her dress that reminded him of the badges Girl Scouts might get. She set the scroll down on the biggest desk near the back wall.

Danny felt a bit sheepish, but he walked closer to her desk station. He took a deep breath and explained. "I'm sorry I left. I was scared. I thought you were going to call security."

She didn't seem upset. If anything, she was amused. Danny was so used to being a disappointment and letting people down that he wasn't ready for how understanding this girl was. "Well, we *did* have to call security since you took the book."

"I didn't take it," Danny said quickly. Then he paused. If this girl rejected him like the others, he had nowhere to go and no one else to turn to. "At first, I thought that my foster brothers had pulled a prank on me. They do things like that. But they wouldn't have had a chance to go all the way back inside. Freddy and Teddy are sneaky, but I don't think they know how to pick a lock, no matter how many action movies they watch."

The girl laughed so hard she snorted. "It's a very special book. No amount of lock picking would have gotten them through that glass."

He nodded. He set the book on the table between them. Just when he thought that nothing would happen, the golden arrows shimmered out of thin air. They undulated across the cover to reveal the hidden text once again. The vines twisted around the corners and the star at the center moved like a compass. This time, the golden light moved along the skin of his hands and traveled down his body. It was like touching exposed wire and getting a sharp jolt. Although not painful, it made Danny jump.

"Whoa!" the girl gasped. The light was reflected in her eyes.

"You can see it, too?" He marveled at his own glowing hands before the threads of gold vanished.

"I can. I mean, I used to," she said. Danny thought he could glimpse something sad in her eyes. "When the book was first brought to the library, I could see the arrows more clearly. But it went away after a few days. I tried really hard to make them come back, but nothing worked. Until today." She spoke entirely too fast, like she was sure of every single one of her thoughts and so she had to say them right away.

"Is that going to happen to me?" Danny asked.

"I don't know, but I know someone who might. It's a good thing you came back."

"Wait, who are you?" Danny asked her, curious. "Shouldn't you be at school?"

"My name is Glory Papillon." She smiled like someone who was used to keeping secrets, and she took a seat at the wide desk. "I'm homeschooled. That way I can assist my auntie North and stay in the library after closing hours. She'll be here soon enough. And you?"

"I'm Danilo Monteverde. My friends call me Danny. At least, they would, but I don't have any friends." He kept a hand on the cover of the book. Glory wasn't trying to take it from him. He just felt possessive over it at the moment.

The sound of heavy footsteps made them both jump up.

"Oh no," Danny whispered.

"Don't worry," she said. "I'll take care of this."

The first thing Glory did was call someone she referred to as Auntie North and tell her that she'd found the Ella St. Clay book. Glory recounted everything Danny had told her and what she'd seen. While she was on the phone, Danny tried to calm his nerves by peering around the office. Every book on the shelf looked just as old as his magical book, if not older.

He loved the sound of that. *His magical book.* If only Mrs. Contreras were here so he could prove to her that he'd been right all along.

"I'll see you soon. Love you, too, Auntie North," Glory said, then hung up. The sound of security guards and static on walkie-talkies was long gone. She looked back up to Danny. "Where were we? Oh, yes. Your friends call you Danny. Well, I'll be your friend."

A friend. He beamed at her. No one had ever *wanted* to be his friend.

"Thank you. I need help. I'm not sure what to do. No one else would believe me about—what we just saw."

Why was he afraid to say it out loud? Did it have something to do with the fact that he'd kept his belief in magic a secret for so long?

"I happen to believe in many things," Glory told him.

"You believe in—in magic?"

"Of course, silly. That's why you're here, isn't it?"

"I'm not supposed to. Believe, that is. My social worker used to make me say that magic wasn't real every day."

She shrugged and had a skeptical look in her eyes. "I'm not supposed to eat ice cream for dinner, but I do it anyway."

"Magic isn't like ice cream," Danny said.

"But ice cream is definitely its own kind of magic." That made Danny laugh for the first time that day. Glory continued, "And so is this book. The arrows revealed themselves to you. That means you're special, Danny."

Special? No one had ever used that word to describe Danny. He was an ordinary boy without a family. A boy who always got in trouble because no one in the entire world wanted to take the time to understand him. Sitting in front of Glory Papillon, he finally felt seen.

"What do you mean by *special?*" he asked.

Glory spun around in the squeaky leather office chair. "What do you know about enchanted books?"

Danny shook his head. He'd heard about witches who had things they called books of cantos and wizards with books of spells, but nothing about enchanted books. "Nothing."

"Some books hold secrets." Glory leaned forward, her voice pitching high with excitement. "Sometimes the secret to making gold out of nothing, or how to cast spells, but the ones Auntie North specializes in are books that turn into maps. Like this one."

"Cool," Danny whispered. "But how does that make me special?"

"Because! The books only reveal their secrets to kids they choose. Kids who really, truly, completely believe in what's inside."

Danny sat back in his chair and gripped the armrests. Even though he wasn't standing, it was like the ground was swaying under him. The room suddenly felt brighter. There was something he hadn't had in so long—hope.

If Pili had also held this book, then that meant the book had also chosen her. He opened the book to the very last page and pointed to the library checkout card.

"What's that?" Glory asked. The girl's eyebrows perked up and she leaned in like she'd been waiting her whole life for an adventure.

"This is my sister's name," Danny said quickly, pointing to the familiar letters. "If you've had this book here, then wouldn't you need a library card to check it out? You need an address for a library card, right?"

"Actually, no. The book isn't logged into any one library. According to Auntie North, every time someone finishes their quest, that kid's name appears on the card."

The hope in Danny's chest felt like it was punched out. "Quest? Then where is she?"

"Wait a minute," Glory said. "You don't know where your sister is?"

He felt himself inhale sharply. He knew she didn't mean to be cruel. She didn't know him or what he'd been through. After two years he could barely say the words: *I don't know where my sister is.*

"She went missing. Everyone convinced me that she was another runaway foster kid. But when we were little, she told me that one day we would find a place where we could have a new home and start over. Somewhere magical." He stopped before he uttered the words *Rio Luna*. "She just vanished. But this card is dated exactly two years ago from today."

Glory picked up a purple pen on the desk and tapped it to her chin, her eyes narrowed in concentration. "How strange."

Strange was one way of putting it. Danny would have said it was totally horrible that he hadn't heard from his sister in two years.

"What's strange? And what kind of quest?"

"Well, usually, the kid who borrows the book returns *with* it."

"I don't understand. Where would she have returned from?" Danny's voice was louder than he meant for it to be. If she'd come back, she would have found him. Even if they couldn't be in the same home for some time, she would have tried to make contact.

"There are so many places to go!" Glory chirped. Orion barked his excitement right along with her. "It says it right here."

They both touched the book between them. The cover

was dull and worn now, but Danny traced his finger where he'd seen the golden letters come alive. He had realized that the star he'd seen wasn't an ordinary star. It was a compass rose that pointed in different directions.

"The book is a map," Danny said. Every nerve in his body felt lit up like Christmas. He was afraid to even say the words, especially after convincing himself that nothing like this could be real.

Glory let out a sharp excited sound. "A map to Rio Luna. If your sister didn't return with the book, then I'd bet my entire library that she's stuck over there."

←9→

The Way to the Siren's Cove

"PILI IS IN RIO LUNA?" he asked. Each word was spoken so carefully it was as if they were made of glass. He reached for the book and flipped to the checkout card again. He wished that Pili's name would light up like the title had. "How do I get her back? How does the book work?"

Glory's eyes brightened, as if she'd been waiting for him to ask. He could tell she liked knowing things. "Remember when I told you archeologists were investigating the Ella St. Clay book?"

Danny nodded.

"My auntie North is one of them. Well, *the* one. There

were others, but they gave up trying to get the arrows to reveal themselves."

Danny thought of the way the golden light had materialized beneath his feet. Now that he knew the truth, he couldn't wait for the next time they'd reappear. "But that's changed now, right? How do I get them to come back?"

Glory bit the inside of her lip and made a thinking sound before answering. "That part I'm not sure of. We've never gotten close enough to the whole map."

"When can we get started?" His entire being was ready to get moving. "If the book revealed itself to me, then that means I can read the map, right?"

"You see this?" She parted the book open and flipped to the end of the first story. There was a rip along the seam where a page had been torn out. "Each story is missing a page. That page is a clue that will piece the map together."

Danny nodded his head. "Like a treasure hunt?"

Glory grinned. "Exactly. When all the pages are returned to the book, we'll be able to enter Rio Luna and look for your sister. That's the heart of this world, and from there you can travel to all the other places, like the Red Woods."

Could this really be happening? He asked, "And the Forever Gardens?"

She nodded emphatically, then sighed. "It's a pity the other archeologists didn't stick around for this. But Auntie North will help us."

"There are adults who believe in magic?" Danny asked. He imagined telling Mrs. Contreras about everything he'd learned that day. Maybe there were some people who couldn't believe, no matter how much proof they had.

Glory seemed surprised. "Why wouldn't they? My auntie North always says she's seen it all and that includes magic. She travels all over the world. Sometimes she takes me with her. Though most of the time she's busy digging up old pottery and weapons—stuff left behind by ancient civilizations."

"You do that?" he asked. He hadn't even thought that was a job someone could have. Well, except for Indiana Jones.

"Auntie North digs. *I* do my homework."

"But, Glory," Danny said. "You saw the golden arrows, too. Don't you already know what the map is?"

Glory shook her head and cast her gaze down. For the first time since he'd known her that day, she looked truly disappointed. "Yes, I could see the arrows. But only for a few days. That's why my name never appeared on the check-out card. I didn't complete my quest."

"What happened?" Danny thought about what it would be like to see magic in front of him and then have it gone. He'd be devastated.

"I'm not sure. One day, we were trying to piece together the first clue. I was the only one who could see the enchantment, so everyone working on the project asked me a lot of questions. Auntie North said that I got so overwhelmed it must have affected my ability to see the arrows. I believe. I know I do. But at that time, I was still thinking about the accident that killed my parents. I had only been living with Auntie North for a year, and discovering that the book had chosen me was the best thing that could have happened. But even with magic around me, I was sad. And then it was gone, and I didn't know how to get it back. Anyway, Auntie North has kept working."

"I lost my parents, too," Danny said. He knew how difficult it must have been for Glory to share that with him. He didn't remember his parents. He'd been too small when he and Pili were put in the System. The only family he'd ever needed was Pili. "My sister was all I had. That's why I have to find her."

"We will." Glory sounded so sure. He wished he could

borrow some of her confidence for himself. "My auntie North will know what to do."

They shared smiles of understanding. Maybe Danny was not as alone and lost as he thought he'd been. Not anymore.

Just then his stomach growled painfully with hunger. In fact, it growled so loudly the entire room seemed to echo. The last thing he'd eaten was the brown bag lunch, and he didn't even get to finish it because of the twins.

"But first, we eat." Glory giggled, and he could feel his cheeks burn red.

"I don't have much of an allowance. None, actually. I saved up a few dollars from helping the neighbor cut the grass."

"I can share mine with you."

Danny's cheeks felt like the time he accidentally ate a blob of spicy wasabi thinking it was a piece of avocado. He didn't want to be an imposition, but he also couldn't deny that he was still hungry.

"Are you sure?"

"Definitely," she said. "Auntie North is in a meeting, so I'll order in, and you can tell me more about you and your sister. Especially if we're going to work together to figure out the map."

"We can *eat* in the library?"

"As long as we stay here."

For a moment, Danny was overcome with too many feelings. He was relieved. He didn't want to go hungry. Running away wasn't exactly a planned decision. But here, in this secret room, he didn't feel so lost. If everything happening was a puzzle piece, they were slowly clicking into place. There was something about Glory. She was a stranger, and yet, he trusted her more than he did anyone else with the exception of Pili.

"Have you ever had ramen?" Glory asked.

"No, but I'll try anything. Today was supposed to be broccoli casserole night."

They both wrinkled their noses.

Glory busied herself on her phone app and because Danny had no idea what ramen was, he let her pick something out for him. The only takeout the Garners liked was Pizza Hut because it was Teddy and Freddy's favorite.

"What is this room, anyway?" Danny asked. "It doesn't look like the rest of the exhibit rooms in the library."

"It's Auntie North's office. She lets me do my homework here. Lately she's been so busy, I spend all night here until she's done with work. Things have been quiet. There isn't a lot of information about Ella St. Clay. Who she was or why she wrote this book. Sometimes it helps finding things out about the author to search for clues. You must see magical things all the time if you were deemed worthy by the book."

"This is the first time I've seen the arrows," he said.

Glory flipped open a notepad with a metal spiral. She tapped her purple gel pen on the surface and waited for him to speak. He felt like he was being interviewed. He wanted to tell her everything. About the dark shapes he thought he sometimes saw, but they couldn't be related. Could they?

There was only one way to find out.

"Sometimes I see shadows moving," Danny said. He winced, like he was ready for her to laugh at him or tell him he was crazy. But that moment never came.

Instead, Glory made a small gasping sound that made Orion bark in his sleep. "I've never seen moving shadows before. Were they scary? I've read that they kidnap kids into other realms to steal their skin."

Danny yelped. "I've never read *that*."

"Well, it depends on who is telling the story. Don't you remember the Shadow Queen in Ella St. Clay's book?"

Danny hadn't considered that before. "I guess I thought any way of getting to Rio Luna would have been better than the alternative."

Besides, he'd been more curious about the shadows than *afraid*. There were so many other things to be scared of, like Freddy and Teddy's pranks, or Mr. Garner's angry fits, or the possibility that he'd never find his sister.

"The scariest part was thinking that I was imagining things. I hated doubting myself."

"We must be very careful from now on. Not all shadows are friendly," Glory said gravely. "The good thing about knowing magic is real is that you'll be able to recognize it more."

Danny decided that he liked Glory and hoped they'd be friends for a long time. He withdrew his hand sanitizer from his backpack to get ready for their delivery. It was nearly empty, so he fished around for the spare.

"Why do you have so many hand sanitizer bottles?" Glory asked.

"The boys I live with, the Garner brothers, they like to stick their slimy boogers and chewed-up gum everywhere."

Danny twisted his face into a grimace at the memory of finding a large piece of gum on the back of the remote control.

"Gross!" Glory exclaimed, but then softened her voice. "You live with a foster family?"

"Yes, but they won't miss me." Danny remembered what Teddy had said. *He's not my brother.* They didn't want him. He would rather be here with Glory and Orion than back in the Garner house. Would anyone show up looking for him? Mrs. Contreras would be so disappointed when she found out what Danny had done . . .

A short while later, their delivery arrived. Danny and Glory feasted on salty ramen. Danny didn't have a name for everything in the soup bowl, but he recognized noodles, corn, and soft-boiled eggs. Glory liked her ramen with lots of chili oil, but Danny decided he needed to start things slow. They shared fried pork dumplings in a sweet black sauce, and Glory even tried to teach him how to use chopsticks. It was hard at first, but he got the hang of it.

"I wish my sister were here," Danny said, slurping up the shortest noodles. "She'd love this."

"You must miss her," Glory said. "What was she like?"

It had been so long since someone had asked him to talk

about his sister. It felt like the whole world had wanted him to forget his family and "move on." So when he talked about her, it felt like unboxing his very best memories of her. Where to even start?

"Pili is the kindest and bravest person I know. I don't really remember our parents, but she did. She's two years older, so she was always in charge. One time, they wanted to separate us, but Pili wouldn't do it, even if it meant that we had to stay in the group home. At least we were together. She's the one who used to read to me. I always had a hard time sleeping, and it was the only thing that would help. She's the one who always took care of me. I haven't seen her in so long, and I'm scared I'm starting to forget her. The way I forgot what my parents looked like. And even looking at pictures doesn't help because they look like strangers."

"Sometimes I feel like that about my parents," Glory said.

"What do you do?"

"When I miss them, I remember everything I can and those memories come back into focus."

Danny felt a well of gratitude fill his heart. For the last two years, being alone was like being in a very dark cave. Talking to Glory, the cave filled with light. He could breathe more easily. Was that sensation also magic?

Just then, *The Way to Rio Luna* by Ella St. Clay shimmered with a faint golden glow. Danny and Glory nearly dropped their chopsticks and stared at the way the book snapped open on the table. There was a halo of light around it. Danny thought it looked like the edges of a sunrise. Neither Danny nor Glory spoke as the arrows raced across the pages. They turned them until they got to the end of the first story.

"Is it trying to tell me something?" Danny asked.

But before Glory could answer, the zigzagging arrow blew up into a shower of sparks. Danny grabbed for it, but his hand closed around air.

"Come back!"

"Don't worry, Danny. We're just getting started."

"Do you really think we'll get to Rio Luna?" Danny asked quietly, almost too afraid to ask the question aloud.

"Indeed we will," a soft and deep voice came from the doorway. "It's a fairyland like no other."

It was a woman with warm tawny skin flushed pink at the cheeks, as if she had just been running. She was dressed in a bright blue pantsuit and cheddar-yellow shoes smudged with dirt at the base. Her deep auburn hair was pulled up in an elegant ballerina bun. She stepped into the room. She pulled up her sleeve to reveal a large watch with dozens of arrows that seemed to move in various directions.

"Auntie North!" Glory exclaimed, standing up. "You're finished early. This is my friend Danny."

Auntie North arched her eyebrow at Danny, then at the book on the table. He wasn't scared of her exactly, but there was something severe in her pale green eyes that made Danny sit up straighter and brush his hair away from his eyes. She was nothing like any librarian or grown-up he'd ever seen.

"So you're the boy who caused all the commotion earlier," she said with a smile.

Danny knew Mrs. Contreras would tell him to remember his manners. "Yes, ma'am."

Glory launched into a long explanation of everything Danny had told her. So much had happened in one day that he was beginning to feel exhausted. He couldn't even believe he'd been brave enough to run away. He was brimming with questions of his own, like how Auntie North had found out about the existence of enchanted books. But Auntie North held her hand up, and the two of them quieted.

"This is all marvelous news! Really the break we've been looking for." She checked her watch. "Come, children.

We must hurry on to the Siren's Cove. Worry not, Danny. We have all the tools there to help us find the answers that must be troubling you."

Danny wondered how she could possibly know everything he was thinking, but he remembered what Glory had said about her aunt having seen many things. Maybe she was used to runaway kids who could see the magical enchantments in books. He packed up his things and followed along with Glory, Orion, and Auntie North. Never in his whole life had an adult believed him so willingly, so quickly. It didn't feel real, and so he pinched himself. That definitely hurt.

As they walked out of the library and to the train station, Danny couldn't help but wonder, how in the world could the subway take them to a place called the Siren's Cove?

To Danny's surprise, the Siren's Cove was five stops away on the B train. Danny had only been on the subway one time and certainly not in the evening. There were so many people in one place all at once. There was a group of men strumming guitars, a pregnant woman balancing a book on her baby bump, businesspeople typing at lightning speed on their phones, and a man with a cat perched on his head. The cat slept, even as Orion lifted his ears and turned his nose in the direction of the feline.

"Be nice, Orion," Glory whispered in his ear, and the young pup settled on the floor in front of them.

Danny marveled at the artwork in the subway station as they emerged somewhere called the Upper West Side. Mr. Garner was wrong. Manhattan was not filled with trash. Well, there was *some* litter here and there. But for the most part, the city was the coolest place he'd ever been to. Across the street was Central Park and the Museum of Natural History.

"I've always wanted to visit," Danny said, trying to keep up with how quickly Auntie North and Glory walked. "My class was supposed to go last year, but Freddy flushed my permission slip down the toilet and I had to stay in the school cafeteria."

"How rude!" Glory turned her frown into a smirk. "Wait until you get to the Siren's Cove. It's filled with just as many wonders. The museum even calls Auntie North to buy or loan things from her, isn't that right?"

"That's right."

"I've never met an archeologist before," Danny said.

Auntie North smiled at him. "Rest assured, not everyone in my field is lucky enough to find the artifacts I do."

"Why's that?" Danny asked.

"Because they're trying to dig up the past to put it in display boxes. I'm trying to unearth magic."

Orion pulled on his leash and tried to run out of Glory's hand. Danny and Glory ran up ahead and gave the dog chase. He crouched down on his paws, his nose sniffing the pavement.

"He likes to play with the mice," Glory said.

Danny wanted to say "gross," but then he realized Orion hadn't found a mouse at all. There was an arrow spinning around in a circle. Orion chased it so they were both like little tornadoes on the sidewalk. The sharp clicking sound of Auntie North's heels was right behind them.

Then the arrow was gone, in a blink of an eye.

Danny nearly tripped over his own feet as he stopped and pointed. "Did you see that?"

Glory had a wonderful grin on her face, her eyes so wide Danny thought they might freeze that way.

Auntie North tapped her chin with her elegant finger. She had the kind of face that wouldn't blink if a spaceship landed in front of her and a herd of chickens flew out the door. All she said was "Fascinating."

Fascinating wasn't the word Danny would have used.

He would have gone for *Weird* or *Am I dreaming again?* or *What is happening?*

"Where did it go?" Danny asked.

"I believe that's got to do with me," the archeologist said. The arrow *did* vanish earlier when Auntie North had entered the room.

"Grown-ups can't see the map enchantments," Glory said. "Even when they believe in the magic within."

"I'm afraid that's the cost of growing up," Auntie North said.

"That doesn't seem fair," Danny said.

He thought of Mrs. Contreras. She had a heart so big, it had enough room for every kid she cared for. If she weren't a grown-up, could she believe? What if adults stopped believing in magic because they were always discouraged by others? It was a dizzying thought.

"We best get inside and go over everything we know."

Auntie North glanced around as they stopped in front of an old brownstone covered in thick ivy. There was *so much* ivy that it covered the hinges and top corners of the door but left the numbers *111* visible.

As they approached, Danny could see the knocker was

shaped like a gargoyle head. Its mouth was wide open, and there was a metal ring nestled around it. Danny wondered if they got many trick-or-treaters.

Auntie North fished in her blazer pocket and withdrew an old-fashioned brass key. Danny had only ever seen skeleton keys like that in old books and movies. She pushed the keyhole cover to the side, inserted the key, and turned it left three times.

"Here we are," she said, and winked at Danny and Glory over her shoulder. "Welcome to the Siren's Cove."

←10→

The Calm Before the Quest

It was when the door opened that Danny could see the plaque above the door numbers. A dull bronze oval that read THE SIREN'S COVE was nailed to the top of the door.

Glory picked up Orion as she crossed the threshold. "We leave our shoes at the front door. Orion is still learning to clean his paws before entering so we have to set an example."

Danny wiped his feet on the mat, which read AHOY!

"Welcome to the Siren's Cove," Glory said, and Orion barked the same.

"I didn't know you could name your house."

"It makes it easy to name our Wi-Fi." Glory chuckled and locked the door behind them. "When I was a little girl, I really loved mermaids. Auntie North used to tell me this story about a lagoon of mermaids that guarded the world's most precious secret. When I moved to Siren's Cove, I pretended to be a mermaid who guarded all of Auntie North's treasures."

"It's wonderful," Danny said. It was more than wonderful. It was everything he'd ever dreamed of seeing in a home. Already, the thought of leaving anguished him. But he followed Glory into an open living room.

Danny took his first step with caution. Every time he walked into a new home, he liked to observe everything about the house. The way the families kept their jackets piled up in the entry hall, or the family photos that cluttered every wall, or the way the food smelled (sometimes like rotten eggs) when he got close to the kitchen. It was Danny's way to see if he could live in a house for a long time. Though none of that mattered with the Garners because he'd known it wouldn't last. For a moment, Danny wondered if they'd noticed he was gone yet.

The thought vanished as he walked into a corridor. A lightbulb hung from a long wire in the ceiling. He knew being in the Siren's Cove was just temporary, but he couldn't stop himself from loving everything he saw. The entrance hall wallpaper was an entire blue-and-white ocean. Waves and waves undulated down an entire corridor. Mermaids, manatees, whales, turtles, eels, pirate ships, and all sorts of sea life were printed on it. Pili would love it just as much as he did, if not more.

Danny kicked off his shoes and set them neatly beside Glory's Mary Janes and Auntie North's heels. There was a bin of umbrellas in all sorts of patterns. Up ahead, an old staircase led upstairs. The wood was peeling in some places, but a string of flamingo-shaped lights was wrapped around the banister, illuminating the hall in a faint pink shine. Glory led him through the entryway.

He turned to look back only once. There was no place he would rather be. With the magical map and his new friends, he was the closest he'd ever been to Pili since she'd disappeared. Despite all that, he was a little bit afraid. What if all of it turned out to be some elaborate joke? What if he was dreaming? What if in the morning Auntie North turned him over to Mrs. Contreras and back to the group home? Or worse, he'd have to go back to the Garners? Danny took a deep breath and tried to steady himself. Pili was in Rio Luna. He had to be brave for her. For both of them. He had to get to her.

The brownstone building was practically a labyrinth. The second he turned right, there was another narrow hallway.

The artwork hanging on these walls was familiar. He recognized some scenes from his favorite stories. There was the Mad Hatter's tea party. There was a young pirate staring up at the stars, a hook for one hand. There was a girl opening the door to a secret garden. Each one was in a separate gold frame. Then there were others he'd never seen before: a large rabbit with horns and a golden crown. A bright green city on the clouds. One painting showed a forest of black trees with leaves as red as blood. There was a lagoon full of mermaids. The last one showed a tall lumberjack with bright petals covering the skin of his arms.

"Here we are," Glory said, and gripped the door handle. Everything in the Siren's Cove looked like it could have belonged to an old fairy-tale castle, including the dragon-headed door handles. "This is where Auntie North and I go over her research. I've been reading older fairy-tale books that are said to be maps to other fairylands."

Glory opened the door. Danny's heart could have stopped

right then and there. He'd never seen so many books in someone's home. The walls had built-in bookshelves. Glass trinkets lined the empty spaces. There was a rolling ladder attached to the bookshelf, and Danny wanted to ask if he could slide around on it the way Belle did in *Beauty and the Beast*. The thing about this room was that the books didn't stop on the shelves.

There were stacks of them atop marble side tables and windowsills. When there was no surface available, the books formed pillars almost as tall as Danny and Glory combined. It was like walking through a city of books. He wanted to reach for one but thought it was better not to touch anything until he was invited. Besides, he didn't want anything to topple over.

Over by a large fireplace was an axe with threads of bronze etched around the handle. It was early September, and though the weather outside was perfect, the Siren's Cove was extra drafty. Auntie North was busy building a fire. The only fireplace Danny had ever seen in someone's house had been at the Finnegans'—but theirs had expensive fake logs that ran on electricity and had flames on a screen.

It was difficult to tell who was more excited—Danny, or Glory watching Danny.

"What's that?" Danny pointed to the items on the fire-place mantel. They were held up by black metal stands.

"Those are Viking drinking horns. They're made from real horns and they're hundreds of years old. They're from Valhalla."

"The heaven of Norse warriors?"

Glory shrugged. "Sadly, no. Just Valhalla, New York. We got them from an antiques collector."

Danny still thought they were cool. The only thing he'd tried to collect were stamps, but then Teddy licked all of them and they lost their value.

Danny turned slowly in a circle and noticed a hunting bow as long as his body. There was an entire display case filled with daggers encrusted with opulent jewels. Necklaces with tarnished metal. It was exactly like being in a museum. Better, even, because he didn't have to crowd in line or be hurried away after a single glimpse.

He pushed up his sleeve and pinched himself. Yep, it hurt. This was really, really real.

Glory went over to a large leather couch and sat down. She set her backpack against the coffee table in front of them. (There were fewer books on the coffee table than anywhere else.)

"Come sit," Glory said, "make yourself at home."

Everyone said that. *Make yourself at home.* The thing was, for Danny it really meant something. He could see himself sitting in one of the tall chairs in front of the fireplace. He could see himself watering the plants strung on the tall windows. He could see himself opening the door to find Pili standing on the other side. Danny sat beside Glory. Every question he wanted to ask felt trapped in his chest like an anxious breath.

"There we are," Auntie North said, dusting her hands as she stood over the crackling fire. "Now all we need is an evening snack and we will get all of this sorted."

"How long before we can get to Rio Luna?" Danny asked. "I mean, if Pili never came back, that means she's over there. But it's been two years. Anything could have happened during that time."

"Time works differently in some fairy realms," Glory said thoughtfully. "A year here could be two weeks there."

Danny stared into the fireplace. A cold sensation crept over him. "What if Pili doesn't even realize she's been gone for so long? What if something happened?"

"Don't worry, Danny," Glory said. "I'm sure Pili is all right. We'll get to her."

It was a funny thing. The moment someone said, "Don't worry," Danny instantly wanted to worry. It felt obvious to him, but he'd never been in this situation before. In this case, Glory and Auntie North were the experts. He would still worry, but only just a little bit less.

He brought out Ella St. Clay's book and rested it on his lap. There was something comforting about the volume, even more so than the copy he had read a hundred times. It felt old and special. Magical. His sister had once held it and found her way to Rio Luna like they'd pinky sworn. He just wished he knew why she hadn't gone back for him first.

"Here we are," Auntie North said, returning with a tray full of delicacies—little cakes and colorful cookies. Beside them was a porcelain pot of tea and three little cups. She set it on a small coffee table and sat on the tall leather armchair beside them.

Danny had never had tea before, but he watched Glory fill her cup with tea, and then add milk and cubes of sugar. It was one of the most wonderful things Danny had ever had. They ate and ate. The cakes were the very best part, full of custard and drizzled with caramel and honey.

"I'm sure you have many questions, Danny," Auntie North said.

"Yes, Miss North," he said. "I mean, ma'am."

She used a tiny metal spoon to stir the sugar in her tea. "My name is Leanna Renee North, but you may call me Auntie North, or Ms. North, if you'd like."

"Thank you. Um. Auntie North, if you can't see enchantments, how did you find Ella St. Clay's book?" Danny asked her. "I thought the arrows only appeared to kids like Glory and me."

"You're correct, Danny. This particular book was found during a dig, actually," Auntie North told him, sipping her tea calmly, though her foot was bouncing a bit. "Up in the Cloisters in Fort Tryon Park. There had been a secret room that no one else had noticed. I specialize in curious and rare objects and one of my colleagues called me right away."

"I was with her," Glory said, jumping into the conversation. She copied the way her aunt held her tea. "It was right after my parents— Well, you know. I didn't want to stay inside the house even though it was cold out. I was sitting in the garden courtyard by myself when I saw the same golden arrows you did. At first, I thought it was a trick of the light. But then I followed the arrows to the room where Auntie North and the others were working." Her smile vanished, and Danny wished he knew a joke or something that would make her laugh again. But he understood the disappointment Glory was feeling because he'd felt it so often.

"*The Way to Rio Luna* did appear to my Glory," Auntie North said. "However, the official statements have to say that the book was discovered in the hidden room of the building. Not all people believe in magical things the way we do, Danny."

He could understand that feeling. It was like being able to hear music that no one else could. Now he wasn't so alone in that.

"The book chose you after Pili?" Danny asked.

A sad smile tugged at Glory's lips. "But after a few days the arrows were gone, and we couldn't put together the map."

"It's all right, my Glory," Auntie North said, reaching out to brush the girl's shoulder gently. "We have Danny now."

Auntie North sat her cup down and locked her pale green eyes with his. Danny felt the need to straighten his posture again. "There are books out there that hold magnificent secrets. Some of them are literal doors to other worlds, while some act as maps. Did you know that the greatest fairy tales and myths ever told have a bit of truth to them?"

"All of them?" Danny thought of the stories he'd

read—of lands brimming with impossible magic. The mermaids of the lagoon in *Peter Pan* and the enchanted island of Avalon from the legends of King Arthur. He imagined the color and chaos of a tea party in *Alice's Adventures in Wonderland*. Was everything he'd believed in true?

A voice in his head answered. *Yes, you know it to be true.*

"How does it work?" Danny asked. "What makes one book a door and another a map?"

Auntie North took a sip of her tea. "Among my colleagues we have a theory. While not every book is a physical gateway to another universe, the ones that are have one thing in common. The authors once traveled to the same enchanted lands they wrote about."

"Is it all one big fairyland, then?" Danny asked.

"Oh, no," Glory said. "Some lands are connected. Others have their own realms. The fairyland of Ella St. Clay's book is an entire kingdom divided into regions. It's named after Rio Luna because the river is the heart of the magic. I'd spend my whole life exploring it if I could get there."

"I think you'd get along with Pili," Danny said with a grin. "What are the other realms?"

"J. M. Barrie was swept to Neverland because he was snatched from the countryside by a shadow," Auntie North said. "Hans Christian Andersen bartered with a mermaid who lived in the cold waters of the Odense Fjord."

"Did you know," Glory said, "sometimes after children return from a magical land, the things from those worlds try to drag them back."

Danny felt something cold in his gut. He didn't like the sound of that. "Like what?"

"Oh!" Auntie North snapped her fingers like she was trying to bring a memory forward. "There used to be a very old journal kept in the British Museum written by Lewis Carroll. He wrote that soldiers from the Red Queen's army came looking for him after he published *Alice in Wonderland*. There is also a record that some of the mermaids from the Neverland lagoon came searching for J. M. Barrie, but the Thames was so polluted, they returned on their own!"

"Why don't more people know about this?" Danny asked, feeling almost outraged. If the world knew that these stories were based on truth, then kids like Danny and Pili wouldn't be told they were mad.

"You see, Danny, as time goes by, some stories are forgotten. Some are kept secret because now that there is very little magic in this world, regular people, the magic-less, wouldn't know what to do with it. Sometimes, like with your sister and the other children who took up the quest of Ella's book, and like you, the magic still finds them anyway. That kid is trusted with something great."

"So it's better to keep these worlds secret?" Danny said. He brushed his palm over the surface of the book. If Ella St. Clay had meant for these stories to be seen only by some, then he was proud Pili had been one of them. Now it was his turn. "And Ella St. Clay went to Rio Luna?"

"She did," Glory chimed in.

"After their visits to these magical lands, the children returned with memories. Then, as adults, those memories faded and became dreams. Some wrote about the things they'd seen and experienced."

"If they can't remember, then how are the maps and portals created?" Danny asked.

"Glory, why don't you answer this one?" Auntie North said. "Let's see how closely you've been paying attention."

Glory cleared her throat. She straightened and her curls shimmied. "Certain authors brought back more than memories. They brought magic with them. We can't be sure what, but we know that for Ella St. Clay, she brought back ink. That enchanted ink was how she wrote this very edition of *The Way to Rio Luna*. All the other copies were reproductions."

Danny looked at Auntie North. "How do you know this?"

She smiled, and her green eyes reminded Danny of glass marbles. "Because when I was a little girl, my mother was ill. My father took us to the countryside while she got better. There was nothing but a pond, a cottage, and an overgrown garden. I found a book hidden under the ivy. When I read it to the very end, it revealed to me a key."

"A key to where?" Danny asked.

"A door made of golden ivy. It was an entrance to a place called the Forever Gardens," she said. "My memories are fuzzy now. I didn't stay long. I remember it was the most wonderful place I'd ever seen. But I had to go back to my mother. Only I didn't know that once I'd used the book, it would reset and disappear. Once I grew up, I wasn't able to see the magic arrows anymore."

"But where do the books go?" Danny asked. He looked from Glory to Auntie North for answers. What if *his* book disappeared before he could find Pili? He didn't want to grow up if it meant never being able to see magic again.

Glory shook her head. "We don't know. Everywhere. Nowhere."

"But," Danny started to say as his mind raced. "Why would anyone keep that a secret?"

Auntie North sat back and took another sip of her tea. "Would you trust anyone with such a place? A place that is special and beautiful and full of wonders?"

Danny thought of Freddy and Teddy. They'd probably show up to the Mad Hatter's tea party and break everything. Well, they *might* make good Lost Boys since they liked staying up all night and not listening to their mother. But the twins already had somewhere they belonged, while Danny didn't. The answer was simple.

"No," Danny said. He wouldn't trust them to go there. "But why do you want to go back to the Forever Gardens, Auntie North? Are adults even allowed?"

She barked a laugh for the first time since he'd met her. "Of course we are. It's a funny thing that happens when you get older. Perhaps it's the reason we can't see the enchantments completely or at all. The world becomes a little darker, a little heavier. You don't stop believing, not exactly. You simply forget that there is magic or a better place. But there are adults in this land, after all. For instance, the kings and queens of the Forever Gardens."

"I wish Mrs. Contreras had believed me," Danny said. "I could have found a clue to Pili sooner."

"Now, Danny," Auntie North said. "Don't think that way. It was a field trip that led you here. They say our futures are written in the stars. Well, I can name the stars in their positions, but few can *read* their messages. Everything we do might be leading us to this promised future. The important thing is that you're here now. Together we will find a way."

Danny's tea had gone cold, but he kept drinking it. It wasn't that bad at all because he had other things to be excited about. *The Way to Rio Luna* was going to reunite him with Pili. He was pretty sure even Mrs. Garner's stroganoff would taste good right about now.

"How do we get the map out of the book? The clues could be anywhere."

Auntie North turned to Glory. "Do you care to answer that one, my dear?"

Glory beamed at the attention. "The books are the maps. Each one is different. For Auntie North, the book revealed only one location, and that was the key to the garden. Others can take you to a looking glass or a portal in the sea or have magic hidden from within the pages itself. For *The Way to Rio Luna*, the golden arrows were trying to lead me somewhere, just like they were trying to lead you to go back to the display room when you were going to leave. But before we could figure out where the book wanted me to go, the arrows vanished."

"I wish they would reveal themselves faster," Danny said.

"We'll get there, Danny," Glory said.

But Danny's mind felt like this one time he was on a carousel and the kid manning the controls got distracted and pressed the wrong button. It went so fast, Danny held on for dear life. He felt like he was barely holding on now. Like, what would Pili have done in Rio Luna? Eat toadstool stew with the fairies? Stand under the rainbow-colored waterfalls near the Cliffs of Nowhere? Then he had a terrible thought. What if the reason she didn't come back with the book was because she was happy there without him? That doubt seemed to crack something within him that was full of hurt and loss and fear.

"What if it doesn't work?" Danny whispered.

"It's okay to be afraid," Auntie North said. "Perhaps if you tell us what you're afraid of we can help."

Danny wasn't used to voicing these things. His emotions were gathered in his chest like a ship in a bottle. But he felt safe in the Siren's Cove and with Glory and her aunt.

"Tons of things, actually. That Pili chose to stay in Rio

Luna without me. That I'm wrong and she *is* stuck, but might be hurt over there. That this is all impossible and I'm dreaming." He couldn't believe he'd actually said those words.

Auntie North considered this for a moment. "I understand that fear. Sometimes you never think your wish will come true so it's easier to believe it will never happen at all."

Orion barked as if in agreement, and as excited as they were, Danny and Glory both stifled deep yawns.

"All right, time for bed, you two," Auntie North said.

"But the map—" Glory and Danny said at the same time.

"It will all still be there after a good bath and a night's rest. Your search will be better for it, trust me." Auntie North stood and ushered them back through the labyrinth halls and up the stairs.

Danny froze. The terrible realization dawned on him. He was now a runaway. "What am I going to do? The Garners—Mrs. Contreras—"

"I'll handle it," Auntie North said. "Do you have a number I can call?"

He had a card with emergency contacts in his backpack and handed it over.

"Glory, show Danny where everything is. He can stay in the guest room."

"Yes, Auntie North."

"Good night, my Glory," she said. "Sweet dreams, both of you."

The moment Auntie North returned downstairs to clean up the living room, Danny looked down at his clothes and felt embarrassed. There were grass stains on his knees and dirt stains on his shirt.

"I don't have clothes to wear," Danny said. "Though I do have extra socks."

"I'm positive we have extra clothes for you," Glory said. From a hallway closet, she pulled out pajamas, a towel, and a bathrobe. Danny had never worn a bathrobe before. "We have guests over all the time. Auntie North has an entire room full of clothes from her travels. I'm sure we'll find something that will fit you tomorrow. Take these for now."

In the bathroom, Glory showed Danny how the knobs worked. There were four of them for some reason, and the tub was one of those old kinds that had feet shaped like giant bird talons. The top was shaped like a clamshell that glistened when he turned the lights on. Everything in the bathroom was blue glass and for a moment he thought that this was what it would feel to have a room under the sea.

"Use whatever you need," Glory said. "There are extra toothbrushes under the sink. Your room is at the end of the hall."

Your room. One of the few times Danny had had a room to himself was so long ago. It was almost a terrifying thing to admit that he'd have to sleep in the dark alone. But then he realized that tomorrow morning he wouldn't have to check and see if the twins had booby-trapped the whole place. He would just wake up with kind people, people who believed in magic. As the tub filled with bubbles in rainbow colors, Danny wished he could somehow tell Pili to hold on and wait for him. They were going to make their promise come true. Maybe they'd even be able to explore Rio Luna once they got there. Perhaps Pili would be an expert the way Glory had been nearly an expert at the library.

Danny could have stayed in the bath for hours, but he was starting to get sleepy and his fingers were wrinkled like raisins. As Danny let the water drain away in a swirl of purple and suds, he thought he heard something call out to him. It sounded like the sound a seashell makes when you hold it up to your ear—and a voice, perhaps. He thought it was coming from the drain, but then he realized, perhaps Glory was singing. She seemed like the kind of person who liked singing to herself.

Danny put on his pajamas (they had tiny narwhals printed all over) and his robe over that. He brushed his teeth and walked to the end of the hall, where the last room was marked with a little metal anchor.

His backpack was on his bed, and the book was waiting. There was a small night-light, which cast a golden light as Danny curled up in the softest, most comfortable bed he'd ever lain on.

"I'll find you, Pili," Danny whispered to the dark. He had hope. "I'm on my way."

←11→

The Long Way to the Red Woods

EVEN THOUGH DANNY HAD a room to himself, he could not sleep. Now that the thrill of the day was gone, his mind turned to darker thoughts. He had not seen Pili in over two years. What if she didn't recognize him? What if she was trapped there because she was injured?

The thoughts twisted in his mind and took the gruesome shapes of fun-house mirrors. He tossed and turned. In the middle of the night, every shadow that loomed on the ceiling and walls appeared like hands ready to snatch him away. After his conversations with Glory, he was afraid of the shadows in his room. That hadn't happened before, but everything was different now that he knew Ella St. Clay's book of stories was about a real place. That meant the good creatures of the Forever Gardens *and* the Shadow Queen herself were real.

When morning came, Danny could hardly open his eyes. He couldn't remember when he'd finally drifted off, but it felt like he'd slept a handful of minutes. He could hardly stretch his tired limbs. He wanted to turn over in bed and fall back to sleep, but his stomach had other ideas. It growled at the scent of bacon that wafted up to his bedroom. The chiming sound of Glory's laugh warmed his heart.

He washed up quickly and made his way down into the kitchen. Very much like the rest of the house, the kitchen was cluttered with paintings and artifacts all over the walls. The refrigerator was covered in magnetic farm animals and souvenirs from places Glory and her aunt might have traveled to. There were beach sandals from Puerto Rico and clogs from Amsterdam and a sphinx from Egypt. On the table there was a bowl full of fruits and vegetables, jars of honey and marmalades. Along the walls were topsy-turvy shelves of cookbooks and books about the history of baking and how to be a beekeeper. Orion had dozed off on a plush floor mat. His paws moved in his sleep, and Danny was almost certain that he was dreaming of chasing Central Park mice.

"There you are, sleepyhead," Glory said.

She was cutting her waffles into perfect squares, each pocket loaded with syrup. Her brown hair was parted down the middle and plaited into two French braids. Her blue skirt was matched by a short blazer and a fuzzy pink sweater with rainbow pom-poms all over. Her book pin was still there, only now she had moved it to the collar.

"Is that a pirate hat?" Danny asked, pointing at the hat on the table beside her.

"It's a tricorne," she said. "But pirates used them, too."

"How did you sleep, Danny?" Auntie North asked. Her blouse was a crisp cream color, tucked into smart red trousers.

Danny's sleep had been restless, but he didn't want to complain since he was a guest. He didn't want to lie, either. "A lot better than waking up in the middle of the night to one of the twins drawing on my face with marker. Thank you."

"I wish I'd gotten to those twins," Glory said, raising her fork like she was wielding a sword. "They only act tough because there's only one of you and two of them."

"And they are bigger," Danny added.

"Now, Glory," Auntie North said, "haven't we talked about violence?"

"I *know*, Auntie North," Glory said with a smile as sweet as syrup. "But it isn't fair how they treated him."

Danny couldn't believe someone was standing up for him. He sat beside Glory at the tall breakfast table and thanked Auntie North for the waffles and bacon. Auntie North and Glory seemed to have a morning ritual. They watched the news from a tiny television that looked about as old as Danny and Glory combined.

Danny noticed the way newspapers were stacked all over the kitchen. Some of them were circled with colorful highlighter. It didn't seem like an odd thing to do because Mr. Garner circled the paper when he was searching for horses to bet on.

It was just then that he turned to the small television screen and saw his face in the pixelated picture. He blinked several times before he realized it was his face. His round face, his coffee-brown eyes, his rave black mess of curls, his light brown skin. The picture was a few years old, from the first Christmas he'd spent without Pili. Mrs. Contreras had bought him a new backpack to replace the one that was ripping apart, but nothing could cheer him up.

"You're on the news!" Glory shouted. She picked up the remote and turned the volume up.

A newscaster appeared beside the photo and spoke with a serious frown on her face. "A trip to the library turns into a mystery on this morning's news. Danilo Monteverde was on a field trip yesterday when he seemed to vanish into thin air. He was last seen getting on a bus after a field trip to the New York Public Library at Bryant Park. It was then that his brothers were attacked by a vicious squirrel. I'm here in Staten Island, where Danilo's foster family, the Garners, are busy searching for him."

The camera panned to the Garners. Mr. Garner combed his thinning hair to the side and the twins smirked as they waved to the camera before their dad slightly nudged them from the back and they took on a somber pose. The only one who had an earnest look of sadness was Mrs. Garner.

"What's going through your head at this moment, Mr. Garner?" She turned the microphone over to him.

"We're worried about Danny for sure. It's been tough on our family. I haven't been able to go to work I'm so worried. But we've set up a fund on MegaFundUs that anyone can contribute to."

"They're making *money* off you?" Glory shouted indignantly.

"What about you two?" the reporter asked the twins. "Do you miss your brother?"

"Oh, *yes*," Freddy said. "We don't know what happened yesterday. One moment we were sharing our chocolate bars. Danny loved chocolate. I'm sure when we find him, he'll want a stack of it."

"You should send it us," Teddy piped up. "I mean, uh, send it to him!"

"What do you have to say about the investigation, Mrs. Garner?" The reporter turned to the mother.

Mrs. Garner looked into the camera. Her short brown curls were threaded with white, and her eyes were red at the corners. "Wherever you are, Danny, I hope you are safe and well. That is all I want for you."

Then she started crying. The camera panned back to the reporter, who talked about the police investigation and Amber Alert. "I'm Amalie Averton, reporting from Staten Island. More tonight at six."

For a moment, the three of them sat in the kitchen in total silence. Danny was feeling too many things at once. Anxious because they needed to get a move on to find Pili. Angry that Mr. Garner was going to make a profit. Angrier still that the twins were using this opportunity to get what they want. Sadness for Mrs. Garner, who had always tried her best in a family that didn't appreciate her. He couldn't even tell her that he did care for her.

"Perhaps I should go back," Danny said quietly. He didn't want that. But it would be simple. It would fix one of the many things that appeared to be wrong at the same time.

"You can't!" Glory said.

"We have to respect what Danny wants," Auntie North said. When she reached to brush his hair away from his face, he jumped a bit. Then he calmed under her touch. "But, Danny, I left a message for Mrs. Contreras last night. She must not have checked her messages yet. I'll call again to get this sorted out as best we can."

It was exactly what Danny wanted—needed—to hear. He didn't want to go back to the System or the Garners. Not without Pili by his side. "Thank you. I don't know how to repay you."

Auntie North gave a rare smile. "Don't think about that now. Let's reunite you and your sister first."

"We can't go anywhere with you in pajamas," Glory told Danny.

He felt his cheeks burn with embarrassment. "The clothes from yesterday are dirty."

"Glory, be a dear and find something for Danny to wear," Auntie North said. She gathered a stack of papers from the table and her coffee mug. "I'll be in my office. My presence will only interfere with the enchantment."

Upstairs, Glory sifted through a walk-in closet stuffed with all sorts of clothes and shoes. There were pieces that looked as if they belonged in the Middle Ages, dresses covered in lace and golden thread, feather boas, jackets covered in stripes, canes with metal heads, robes fit for Merlin himself. It was like being in a costume shop.

"Here we are," Glory said, and pulled out a pair of jeans and a T-shirt that looked like a long-sleeved baseball shirt but instead of a team logo, there was a knight brandishing a sword.

She looked at her watch the way he'd seen Auntie North do and said, "Meet you in the living room!"

————

Downstairs, Danny and Glory cleared the coffee table. They opened *The Way to Rio Luna* by Ella St. Clay and carefully leafed through it. The pages weren't as brittle or as old as they looked, which made Danny think that there was definitely some sort of magic laced in the paper or ink. The book contained four stories in total. Each one was decorated with a sketch at the very beginning, which was different from the beat-up copy he'd carried with him everywhere.

"I used to have a copy of this book," Danny said. "My foster father threw it out."

"That's horrible!" Glory said. "I used to have a copy, too. When I went to come and live with Auntie North, there was a flood and some of my boxes were ruined. But isn't it cool, Danny? No one has the original but us."

He knew she was right. They shared something that no one else in the world had.

"How do we start?" Danny asked. "What did you do the first time?"

Glory was holding her purple gel pen and a small notepad. She tapped the pen on her chin and made a deep-thinking sound, then drew a series of arrows on her notepad.

"When the arrows and vines revealed themselves to me, it was when I read the first tale out loud. That's when we discovered that the last page is missing in each story. The enchantment was pointing at the ripped seam and I knew that I had to find it. The gold light moved around super fast at first. They went all over the book's covers, on the ground of the Cloisters, even on my dress. And then"—she snapped her fingers—"the enchantment stopped."

"But why?"

"I don't know. The only problem is, we haven't been able to find anyone who can see the enchantment since me." Glory made a worried face that made them both laugh. "Until we met you."

Danny hadn't seen any arrows since they arrived at the house and suddenly felt a lot of pressure. "What if the same thing that happened to you happens to me?"

"I don't think it will," she said. "I have a good feeling about this."

Danny grinned at her encouragement. He turned to the last page in the first story. The remaining pieces of the ripped page grew out of the spine like a jagged mountain range. "It's sort of like a video game or a quest. Follow the arrows and collect the pages."

It seemed easy enough, but Danny knew how difficult journeys could be.

"Then let's start," he said.

Danny and Glory pulled the book onto their laps between them. He could sense the same spark of magic that he'd had yesterday. It was just beneath his skin where he couldn't scratch at it or pick it like a scab.

The first story in *The Way to Rio Luna* was called "The Moon Witch in the Red Woods." Out of all the stories in the book, this one was Pili's favorite. The drawing at the top was of a young girl with silvery hair and a long red cloak. In her hands was a sickle moon, and behind her was an outcrop of spindly red trees with branches that looked like crooked fingers.

Danny cleared his throat and read.

"'On nights when the moon was nothing but a sliver of a crescent, the gateway between the Red Woods and the mortal world was paper thin. One night a young witch was walking in the wintry woods of her human world when she caught the silver light of the moon shining through a rip between the worlds. It looked like a fissure, an open wound made by someone in a hurry to get out. Only, there was no way to tell which direction they were headed. Still, the young witch realized the moon she was seeing was no ordinary moon. Lured by the promise of magic, she stepped through the portal and into the Red Woods.'"

Danny closed his eyes and remembered the way Pili

used to act out the scenes. She cut out a picture of the moon and pinned it to her shirt like the emblem of a superhero.

"'There, the young witch, named Leigh the Bard, learned to wield the power of the night sky. She pulled threads from moonlight and threaded the magic between her fingertips. Even her hair turned the same silver. It was then that her adventures first began.'"

With each page, nothing happened. Danny tried not to grip the book so hard, but he was nervous. What if it had all been a fluke? The only thing that helped him focus was the words on the page. Though the ink didn't move, he could imagine Ella St. Clay's pen moving furiously across the pages.

He got to the part where Leigh became such a strong witch that she was made guardian of the Red Woods. She helped the fairies and creatures who lived in the dark lochs and in the hollows of trees. She helped the jackalope royal family keep peace in their lands. But the Shadow Queen didn't like these acts of kindness. She wanted every part of Rio Luna under her shadow and began to hunt the Moon Witch. Not only did she control living shadows, she also had the ability to become invisible.

When they turned the following page, they reached the ripped ending of the story. Danny knew how it ended, but felt a twinge of disappointment. The arrows hadn't appeared. Worry sank into him like sharp claws on his chest. Why weren't the arrows revealing themselves to him? When he'd been in the library, the golden light didn't want to leave him alone! Did the magic awaken because he was near? Danny could *sense* the magic back then. He couldn't put words to it at that moment in the library, but he'd definitely felt something strange was happening. He thought back to the exact moments before the arrows materialized. The twins had tripped him, and then he went off on his own. He was angry and wanted to get away. But he'd also made a wish.

He'd wished *more than anything* that Pili were with him. But Danny had wished so many times it felt just like any other thought. What made that day so special? Was it because he needed to be near the book? Was it because finally, after all this time, there were people who encouraged him?

He could feel the magic on his skin again, and in that moment he realized that he was holding his breath. It was like every fear he'd had. Fear of being alone and abandoned was like a wall preventing him from experiencing the magic that had latched on to him. Magic that he'd wished for since he could remember. All the grown-ups had tried to stop him from believing, but now there was no one to stop him.

"I believe," Danny whispered.

A light breeze blew through the living room. It moved the stray curls coming undone from Glory's braids, the curtains, and the leafy plants decorating the wide living area.

The skin on Danny's arms lit up. Golden threads appeared on his skin like leafy vines curling and coiling.

"Whoa!" Glory said, bouncing in her seat beside him. The book began to fall, but Glory caught it.

"What's happening?" Danny shouted. He held his arms up. Was it possible for magic to have a *sound*? A soft chiming filled the room as the light illuminated their awestruck faces.

"You have a tattoo!" Glory pointed at his arms.

She was right. The gold arrows took shape on the tops of his hands. On the left was a crescent moon and on the right was something that looked like an archway made of bricks. There were two words at the center: *the loch*.

Danny touched his skin, tracing the lines of the arrows that swirled in all directions. It was the kind of warmth he felt on a cloudless sunny day. *He* was magic. The only thing that would make that moment better was if Pili were there.

The image on his hand had to be connected to the story. He thumbed back to the beginning.

"What are you looking for?" Glory asked.

"There were lochs in the story," Danny said. He pressed a finger on the page. The Moon Witch lived in the loch of the Red Woods! "Is there a loch in New York City?"

He felt silly asking, because the only loch he'd ever heard of was Loch Ness, where Nessie the Loch Ness Monster was said to live. But Mrs. Contreras had once told him to always ask questions, even if he felt foolish doing so. That was the only way he would learn and get things right.

Glory tapped her chin with her pen again. "*Loch* means lake in Scottish . . . Wait a minute."

She hopped off the couch and darted to the other side of the living room. She rifled through a bin full of tall rolls that reminded Danny of wrapping paper. She seemed to know exactly the one she wanted even though they all looked the same on the exterior. She brought it back to the table, and when she unrolled it, Danny could see a map of Manhattan Island. This version of the city was different— there were strange symbols on the four corners: a crescent moon, a trident, interlocked triangles, and a sun. The buildings were replaced by greenery, and sea monsters undulated across the Hudson River.

The moment he touched his hands to the map, the arrows transferred from his skin and onto the paper. Some were pencil thin, others were made of little dots, and one was like a thick vine of ivy. At the north side of Central Park was a small stream called the Loch and beside that something called Glen Span Arch. The arrows darted across the paper and pointed at it.

"Our first clue," Glory marveled at the moving arrows.

"Here!" Danny said. "This is where we have to go."

"Then that is where we are going," Auntie North said from the door.

The golden light vanished from the map. It was like the time he turned on the light switch on his way to the kitchen, but the bulb blew out. It must feel awful for Auntie North, he considered. He knew what it felt like to know that magic was real and not be able to see it. A sickle moon remained on Danny's left hand. He touched it again, glad for its warmth. It was a promise that things were looking brighter.

Glory grabbed her trench coat and put it on. "Are you ready, Danny?"

"I've never been more ready in my whole life."

12

The Moon
Witch

THE KIDS, THE POMERANIAN pup, and the archeologist set off in search of the first missing page. Danny's insides felt like a soda can that had fallen down the stairs. The sky was overcast and a cool breeze blew green leaves and white spring flowers from the trees. A sparrow flitted by so fast it looked like it vanished into thin air.

Glory held Orion by a leash. Her tricorne hat cast a long shadow around her, but Danny knew she was grinning. Auntie North walked just as swiftly as her niece but glanced over her shoulder every few moments. All around them were people moving to and fro at a superfast pace. He wondered if everyone in New York City walked that fast.

Danny sped up to not get left behind, and clutched his book against his chest. It *felt* like his book. His lifeline to Pili.

Danny kept glancing at his arms. Yep. The golden arrows were still swimming across his skin. One of them leapt off, like he'd seen whales and dolphins do on the Discovery Channel. It landed on the ground. It was helping lead the way. Glory could barely hold on to Orion's leash as he chased after the arrow.

"Why do you keep looking behind you, Auntie North?" Glory asked.

"I want to make sure we aren't being followed," their guardian explained. "Remember, Glory. Magic has a pulse."

"Like a heartbeat?" Danny asked.

"In a way," Auntie North said. "Even grown-ups like me, who might not be able to see magic, can feel there's something around."

"Why is that a bad thing?" He looked over his shoulder, but there were only joggers and horse-drawn carriages around.

Glory leapt over a puddle and stood tall. "Because some

want magic for dark deeds. But don't worry, everyone. Orion will be our lookout!"

They trudged up hills, a cluster of boulders that reminded Danny of a giant taking a nap, then they walked alongside a reservoir, through patches of trees that made it feel as if for a moment they could be in woods like Leigh the Bard in the story. Though he was sure the Red Woods weren't surrounded by skyscrapers the way he was.

"Doesn't that rock formation look like a giant taking a nap?" Glory asked.

"I was just thinking that!" Danny said.

When he peered over his shoulder, he got the sharpest sensation of déjà vu. He'd thought the same thing when he saw it. The *first* time they walked past it.

"We walked in a circle!" Danny said.

"What's happening?" Glory asked.

Before Danny and Glory could start freaking out, Auntie North stepped forward. "We can figure this out. Secret books must remain secret for a reason. Otherwise, everyone could get their hands on them."

Danny took a deep breath and looked at their surroundings. There was a long, paved road where joggers and cyclists moved in two traffic lanes. Enormous trees in full spring bloom. The boulder that looked like a giant. They should be able to *get* to the arch simply by walking. But magic wasn't simple. He had linked together Ella St. Clay's story of the Red Woods with a real location in New York City. What if there was another connection?

"How did Leigh the Bard get into the Red Woods?" Danny asked Glory.

"She saw the light of the moon and that led her there," Glory said. "Moon portals are very rare and only occur in certain places in the world, so we can rule that out. But she did see—"

"A rip," they said at the same time.

Danny and Glory turned to the rock formation. There was a small sparrow perched on the very top, where the giant's ear might have been. It was a curious bird, on closer inspection, with a cluster of red feathers on its belly. Danny remembered the squirrel that had caused the distraction to help him get out of that bus. Was he kind of like Snow White or Cinderella with animals helping him out? The sparrow spread its winds and took flight. It vanished. Now he knew to trust his sight. Earlier, when he'd seen the bird disappear, it wasn't because it flew too fast. Even a bird couldn't fly that quickly. It had *gone* somewhere.

"There!" Danny pointed at the rock formation.

"Let's go," Glory said.

Together, they hurried closer to the sleeping giant. Danny and Glory took turns sticking their hands into the gray rock. Each time their fingers went right through. They must have looked like kids karate-chopping the air.

"What do the arrows say, Danny?" Auntie North said. She stood a few yards away, as if careful to keep her distance.

Danny held out his arms. The arrows all pointed in a single direction now. Straight ahead. There was no physical rip, but that didn't mean that there wasn't anything there. He'd believed in magic way before he could see it was real. He had to trust himself now.

"I think we have to go through the rock," Danny said.

Glory adjusted her hat, but she did not doubt him. "Let's do this."

Danny felt his heart thump. But even Orion barked, and Danny hoped it was encouraging. He shut his eyes and stepped through the rock. It was like walking into a department store and feeling the cold blast of air after a long, hot walk. When he opened his eyes, he was still in Central Park, but a slightly different version. The light around them had a blue tint, and even though the gray sky hid the sun, they could see the clear outline of a crescent moon.

"Wow," Danny whispered.

"Are we still in Central Park?" Glory asked, coming up behind him. Orion followed.

Danny looked over his shoulder. "Where's Auntie North?"

"She's keeping the coast clear," Glory said. "She doesn't want anything to interfere with you being able to see the enchantment. Especially her presence."

They kept going, finally reaching the loch, which had been marked on the old map in the Siren's Cove. Just beyond that was the brick arch mirrored on Danny's right hand. Here the trees were taller and the thick brush of leaves gave them plenty of cover. They climbed down a set of boulders. Orion was so excited, Glory let him off his leash. He barked and cut a path that led to a sandstone archway embedded into a stone wall facing a trickle of stream.

"It looks like a tunnel that's been bricked up," Danny said, trying to catch his breath.

"Hmm," Glory said. "A tunnel has to lead somewhere, doesn't it?"

They pressed their palms to the stone. Danny had hoped the bricks turned into a secret doorway like the sleeping giant, but no matter how hard they tried, it wouldn't give. The stone was warm to the touch, like the sun had been shining on it all day even though thick clouds blanketed the sky. The archway wasn't very deep, and it was paved over with neat rows of stone rectangles.

"Do you hear that?" Glory asked, looking up. Danny listened closely. Beneath the rustle of leaves and the trickle of water from the loch, there was a chime of magic. It moved around them. To the left. To the right. Behind and then forward. It was playing tricks with them. He didn't like the idea of ghosts one bit.

Then came a hard voice. "Why have you come here?"

Danny felt something graze the back of his neck. Was it invisible? If magic was real, did that mean that ghosts were, too? He whirled around. Glory spun so fast her hat came off.

"Who's there?" Glory asked.

Orion barked and barked. He ran from them and leapt into the air. He grabbed something with his teeth and bit into it.

"That dog needs some training," the voice said with a little sniff.

"Why are you doing this?" Danny asked. He felt the breeze again, then saw the sparrow fly by once more.

"The question is, why are you here?" the voice asked.

Danny was about to answer, but Glory interrupted by saying, "I don't know if we should trust this."

"*You're* the one who has stepped into my pocket realm. I should be the one with trust issues," the voice said, getting louder and louder.

"She could be evil like the Shadow Queen," Glory said. "Remember, Danny? One of her powers was invisibility!"

"How dare you suggest I'm anything like that witch! She stole that trick from *me*." The air in front of them rippled like dropping a stone in water. Then she appeared: a young girl with long hair that shone as silver as the crescent moon above. It tumbled down her shoulders in waves and stopped at her waist. Her eyes were just as bright, and her pale skin had a rosy blush on her cheekbones. Her sweeping black dress was covered in silver stars, and a heavy moon pendant hung from a long chain around her neck.

Danny knew who she was almost instantly. "You're the Moon Witch!"

The Moon Witch smirked. Though she appeared to be

in her early teens, there was something about her that made her look ageless.

"I prefer Leigh the Bard," she said, and pressed her hand to her chest. "I *am* a poet first and foremost."

Leigh the Bard looked them up and down. "I see the boy has the mark of the book."

Danny flushed at being noticed. He'd read about Leigh for years, and here she was standing in front of him. He pinched the inside of his elbow and discovered that he was not dreaming. He knew it was rude to stare, but he'd never seen a witch like her before. Or any witch at all.

"If you're here, does that mean other characters from the stories in *The Way to Rio Luna* are here, too?"

She tented her fingers. Her fingernails were metallic rainbows and pointed at the ends. When she tapped them against each other, they made a twinkling sound. "Magic from Ella's book does have a way of finding its way out."

Danny and Glory perked up at the sound of Ella's name.

"You must be the first clue!" Glory said.

Leigh rested her hand on her hip. "I am more than a clue. I am the dialogue between the celestial and the ground."

Danny and Glory exchanged a quizzical stare. He was sure Glory didn't understand what that meant, either.

"Uhh . . . Does that mean you have the missing page?"

Leigh spread her arms out. Her dress sleeves billowed out like bat wings. "I do. But like all the others, you'll have to prove yourself."

"I'll do anything," Danny said. Nothing was going to stop him from finding his sister.

Leigh the Bard raised a finger. "Be careful who you make that promise to. Not all are as friendly as I."

Friendly wasn't exactly the word he'd use. But he was sure of it. He'd do anything. At a loss for words, he just nodded while Glory tried to rein in Orion. The pup came bounding back, jumping excitedly at Glory. There was something in his jaw. For the first time, Danny realized that the Moon Witch had one bare foot, and her silver slipper was covered in Orion's drool. Glory wrestled the shoe back and, holding it by the tips of her fingers, returned it to its rightful owner.

"When I wished for a Cinderella ending, this is not what I had in mind," Leigh told them. "I'm afraid pets are not allowed. A traveler who brought their Doberman once ate one of my manuscripts. Now, follow me . . ."

She turned to the arch Danny and Glory had just been poking and prodding. The very air around them seemed to bend, and an impression on the stone revealed itself where it hadn't been before. Using the moon pendant that hung from her neck, the Moon Witch pushed it into the empty spot. As soon as it fit, the stone turned into a wooden door with fat iron hinges and a door handle. It swung open, and the entrance was bathed in moonlight.

"Come, all who dare! The entryway is enchanted so only those with their shadow intact may enter." Leigh the Bard stood to the side and let the others go first.

Danny had never given too much attention to his shadow. He gulped a nervous knot in his throat, then lifted his feet, and the shadow followed.

One by one, they filed into the small house, their shadows trailing on the ground beside them. Roots stuck out from the ceiling in tangled braids. Orbs of light flitted from one side to the other. Beneath them, smooth stone tiles lined the floor. Night flowers in dark purples and blues sprouted from the vines in the walls and even between the cracks in the wall. Yellow birds the size of baseballs were perched on the backs of chairs, on the rows of bookshelves, on the top of a typewriter nestled on a wooden desk. Danny and Glory marveled at all of it. One of the yellow birds bounced onto a stack of notebooks, while the others lifted modern ballpoint pens and quills with their beaks.

"Excuse me," the Moon Witch said. "It is spring cleaning."

"You live right beneath the city?" Glory asked. She reached for a low-hanging tree root. There was a clump of dirt on the end. When she touched it, the root shook itself and curled back like an octopus tentacle. "*Cool.* And no one has noticed?"

"I find people don't notice many things in this world," Leigh said. She found a new pair of slippers, blue this time, and tugged them on. "Even when it's in front of them. Willie, put the kettle on."

Danny and Glory looked at each other. He mouthed to Glory, "Who's Willie?" Then there was a strange groaning sound, like when Danny stretched after a long, deep sleep. From above, the roots were coming alive like long, twisted fingers. They lifted an iron kettle and set it on the hearth. Danny would have thought a hand made out of bark might be afraid of fire, but it didn't even flinch. Other roots lowered to a small cupboard and grabbed a couple of mugs made from hollowed acorns the size of apples.

Leigh pressed her hand against the wall, where roots grew like spiderwebs against hard-packed earth. "Willie is the tree growing directly above me. They keep my house together, and keep the missing page safe. Not to mention make the perfect cup of tea."

Danny was anxious and wanted to refuse the tea. But he knew that in the story, the Moon Witch loved her teatime with the king and queen of the Red Woods. They took seats on benches made out of tree stumps while Leigh sat on a high-backed chair that faced them. When she moved, it looked like the silver stars were winking. Glory straightened her back and cleared her throat, like she was getting ready to give a presentation in front of the whole class. "Pardon me, Ms. Bard—"

"It's Ser Bard," the Moon Witch said. "I was knighted after defeating the Shadow Queen and leaving her in the tower to wait out her lifetime sentence. But *Ella* didn't include that, did she? It's all right. I've been writing my own version of what happened. Anyway, you were saying— What are your names again?"

"Glory Papillon," Glory said proudly.

"And I'm Danny Monteverde."

The young knight witch smirked and settled into her chair. "Good to meet you. You were saying?"

"Ser Bard," Glory continued, "we're here for the missing page."

"Of course you're here for the missing page! That's what everyone comes here to find, isn't it? No one comes to visit me, or check up on my progress, or asks me to read a couple of pages. No. It's just me and my birds." The walls around them groaned. "And Willie, of course."

Danny winced sharply at that. He recognized the feeling of being alone with no one to talk to.

"Ser Bard," he began to say. "How come you're back in this realm? Why not stay in the Red Woods if you were a guardian and you were knighted?"

Leigh the Bard quirked a brow. She wasn't expecting that question. "After we defeated the Shadow Queen, I was ready to come home. I missed my family terribly. Only, the world was different after I returned. Everyone I loved was gone. I've been fourteen for almost a hundred years now."

"You've been here all this time?" Glory asked.

"I thought of going back. But after so much time here, I couldn't go back to the Red Woods. I've grown up too much. So when Ella created the map to Rio Luna, she tasked me with guarding the last page of my story, and I obliged."

Glory tapped her pen to her chin. Danny hadn't realized she was taking notes. Should he be taking notes? "Who are you protecting the key from?"

Leigh glanced around her small house. The orbs of light shone brighter. When one flew close, Danny realized it was a fairy with a pointy face and blue skin. She smiled with sharp, small teeth, then flitted away when some dirt from the roof fell down on her.

"The shadows, of course."

"I used to think shadows were good. Like friends who carried you away somewhere fun," Danny said.

"Once, maybe," Leigh told them. "But the Shadow Queen . . . She had the darkest heart in the land and she corrupted the shadows. She made them take children from across the realms."

"How did she corrupt them?" Glory asked, wide-eyed.

"Children are a delicacy to the Shadow Queen. There is hope in their eyes. Sweetness in their teeth. Haven't you heard of stories where children are had for supper?"

Danny thought of the story of Hansel and Gretel. He hadn't eaten gingerbread since his sister had read that one to him. Still, everything Leigh the Bard was telling them didn't sound like the Rio Luna that he'd imagined.

"But if you defeated the Shadow Queen, why would the shadows be a threat?" Danny asked.

"Some of them survived and are in this land, trying to

return and once again bring darkness to the regions of Rio Luna. There are portals around the world, hot spots where the veil between the worlds is most thin. Shadows can't access those. But when Ella wrote her book, she used enchanted ink she transformed from the magic of the land's river. It made the book take on a life of its own. It was meant to help other children experience the joy of magic. To guide them. The book finds those with true hearts. Hearts that love. Souls that are kind. Minds that believe. Those are the qualities the magic is attracted to. All a shadow would have to do is hitch a ride with the kid who pieces the map together, and return. That's why I guard this last page."

"Do you remember the last kid who came looking for the missing page?" Danny asked. This was the closest he'd been to Pili in a long time, and he wanted to get as much information as he could.

Leigh tapped her metallic nail on the tip of her chin and nodded slowly. "In fact, I do remember a young girl. About your size. Same black hair and doe eyes like you."

"That's my sister, Pili!" He nearly fell off the stump he sat on.

A gathering of the yellow birds landed on Leigh's shoulder and chirped back and forth. Danny wished he could understand them. It was as if they had their own language.

"I don't remember much, I'm sorry." Leigh shook her head. Glitter fell from her hair. Or maybe it was very fine stardust. "But she did mention a brother she would do anything for. She *was* in a hurry."

Tears pricked at the corners of Danny's eyes. He wished he could tell Pili that he was on his way. "She didn't come back with the book. She's stuck on the other side, and I have to get to her."

"Stuck in Rio Luna?" Leigh the Bard said sharply. "How strange."

Glory drained her tea, and Willie brought down a tree root and took the empty acorn from her hand. "Do you know where Ella is? Maybe we can ask her how someone would get stuck there?"

"I haven't seen her in decades," Leigh said with a touch of real sadness. "But I can get you one step closer to your first missing page."

"I'm ready," Danny said.

"Me too," said Glory.

Leigh raised a single brow and gave them a sly smile. "You'd better be. Each of the four pages creates a very thin crack into fairyland. Just like the one I came through. Ella used that barest gateway, too small to let a whole person through, but big enough to hold a key. You need them in order to get the door. Pili could be anywhere. Rio Luna is full of many wondrous kingdoms."

"That's all right," Danny said. "I just need to get there."

"As you wish," Leigh said. It was then that the Moon Witch set her luminous eyes on the children in front of her. The roots around them groaned and moved. They twisted like ropes of taffy. Dirt fell around them. For a moment, Danny thought there was an earthquake. But then he realized a hand made of roots emerged from the ceiling. Within its grasp was a glass cylinder, and within that was a yellowed piece of paper tied up with a silver string.

Danny reached for it. But when he made to take a step, the roots shot up from beneath. They wrapped around his ankles and shins. He screamed, and beside him, so did Glory.

"What are you doing?" Danny shouted.

Leigh the Bard, Guardian Knight of the Red Woods and Moon Witch, stood. Her dress trailed on the ground. Her birds rested on her shoulders. They chirped loud enough to silence Danny and Glory.

"I told you, I must protect the missing page," she said. "To do that, one of you must do one thing."

"What?"

"Answer a question truthfully. Then, and only then, will the enchantment release you."

Glory grunted and struggled, but the more she fought, the harder the roots tightened around her limbs. "And if we answer wrong?"

"Then you'll be trapped within the tree," Leigh said.

"What do you want?" Danny asked with a groan as he struggled to wrench himself loose.

"You said you'd do anything to get your sister back, Danny. Is that true?"

Danny cried out when the roots twisted around his calves and knees. He had said those words earlier, and he thought he had meant them.

"Can you give up the one you love the most even if it meant stepping foot in Rio Luna?" the Moon Witch said.

"Please," Glory said. "Let us go."

The roots clamped down around their arms and torsos. Danny felt like the air was being squeezed from his chest. But he knew the answer. The words burned on his lips. He'd read enough fairy tales to know that there were hidden meanings in all the words. How could he give up the one he loved the most? That was Pili, and he was trying to get there for her. Even apart, she was always with him . . . Wasn't she?

"What's it going to be?" Leigh waved her finger in the air to mimic a ticking clock.

"That's a trick question," Danny said. "You can never give up the person you love. Because even when they're gone, they're still in your heart."

But the roots kept winding around their throats, their mouths. Danny and Glory let out muffled screams. Leigh the Bard tapped her metallic nail on her chin. Her smile was wide and mischievous.

"Right you are, Danny!" she said, and waved her hand in the air. The yellow birds scattered. "Willie, do let them go before they asphyxiate."

They were freed. Danny's skin was hot and cold at the same time. They fell to the ground, breathing heavily.

"Are you all right?" Danny asked.

"I think so," Glory said, dusting off her clothes. She picked up her hat and righted it.

"Well done," Leigh said. Dirt fell from the ceiling as she

tugged the slender glass tube free from the gnarly hand jutting out from the ceiling. She handed Danny the glass vial. He held it gingerly between his palms. This fragile thing held all his hopes and dreams. It was the best and most terrifying thing to be able to hold it. He had the first missing page. He was one step closer to his sister.

The golden arrows glowed once again. The archway on his right hand was beginning to fade.

"Thank you," Danny said carefully.

"Even if you did try to kill us," Glory muttered.

"I did no such thing," Leigh the Bard said. "You chose to go on this quest, Glory Papillon. You might decide what it is you wish to gain from it."

Glory nodded gravely as the bricks opened up once again to let them onto the park street. The Moon Witch lingered at the door.

"Make sure to remember your true hearts."

"Thank you, Ser Bard," Danny said. "Good luck with your book."

When they turned around, the wooden door became stone, and the archway had sealed itself once again. The crescent moon shone overhead, and the blue light of the day made it seem as though nothing had changed.

"Are you sure you're okay?" Danny asked.

Glory gave a small nod. She plucked a tiny twig stuck in one of her French braids. "Why wouldn't I be? We have the missing page! Come on."

Danny couldn't help but feel that she wasn't being honest. How many times had he told Mrs. Contreras he was feeling all right when he really wasn't? But he followed after Glory back through the stone. The cold sensation washed over him again as they stepped into a now-sunny Central Park.

←13→

The Surprise Visitor

AUNTIE NORTH AND ORION were waiting for them. She was reading on a bench. It was so bright that for a moment it looked like neither of them had a shadow. Then Orion leapt forward, and Danny could see it was only the angle they were sitting at.

"We have it!" Glory said. Danny held the glass tube in the air. "The first clue to Rio Luna!"

"Well done," Auntie North said. Orion barked his approval. He ran into Glory's arms and her mood brightened instantly.

"Open it!" Glory exclaimed.

"Perhaps we should get somewhere a bit more private?" Auntie North asked. She took out a pocket watch and flipped it open. "The Ravine will do this time of day."

Danny held the glass tube with great care as they walked. Glory went over every detail of their encounter with the Moon Witch. Auntie North apologized for not having anticipated that kind of challenge. At least they'd be prepared for the next time, even if Glory did have to pull out two splinters from her palms.

They reached the Ravine moments later. The new leaves on the trees were bright green. Though now Danny could never look at tree roots the same way again. There was a small waterfall and nothing else but the sound of water and the breeze. Even the traffic was muffled here. They kept to the shore and gathered around.

He brushed the dirt away from the glass. He unstoppered the top and removed the scroll. The paper was soft and smelled like an old library. Danny wondered if the whole park could hear the sound of his heart. He'd met a character from his book. Sure, she'd tried to crush him with Willie, her magic tree, but Leigh the Bard had also helped him.

Danny pulled the string around the scroll and unfurled it. Instantly, he recognized the magic within. Though the gold markings were fading from his skin now that they'd accomplished their first task, it was the same magic that was in the paper. In the ink. Ella St. Clay had taken magic from Rio Luna to give kids like him the opportunity to dream. He was so excited he was afraid he might crush the paper from holding it so tightly.

Slanted, elegant letters filled the page. It was ripped at the exact angle as the first missing page in the book. When he returned the ending to the story, the golden thread returned and stitched the page back together. Danny blinked a few times, because the ink on the page was illuminated from beneath, just as the first time he'd laid eyes on the book.

"What do you see?" Auntie North asked, leaning closer to the book. There was a shine in her eyes, like she was so thrilled she could cry.

"The words are turning gold," Glory said. She held her hands to her chest as if she might burst, and Orion barked and barked.

Danny watched the ribbons of gold glisten. He read the words that jumped out. The book had revealed its secrets, after all.

The road to the Red Woods is paved with starlight.

The spring air was crisp, and the sound of laughter from

the nearby streets made its way to them. Perhaps he needed to read the rest of the page. *Something* should have happened by now, but they kept waiting.

"Come on," Danny said, the familiar sensation of disappointment brewing in his heart. He couldn't come this far only to fail.

In that moment, a great light burst in front of them. One time, during the Fourth of July when he was six years old, Pili had used her birthday money to buy a box of sparklers. She and Danny lit them up in the backyard of their group home. Pili shared them with the other kids, and they ran around waving the sparklers in the dark.

That's what these gold lights looked like. The space in front of them was now a sheer wall.

"Are you seeing what I'm seeing?" Danny asked. His belly flip-flopped like he was on a roller coaster.

"We are," Glory said in wonderment. She took Danny's hand in hers.

As the ripple stopped, the surface became more like clear glass. At the center was a flat metal piece stuck between the clear wall separating this world and Rio Luna. Danny could see straight into the other side. There were hills made entirely of black grass. There was a narrow path that cut through the land and led to a forest of black trees with bright red leaves. A strong breeze moved through the woods, and a tremble rebounded across the hills. The sky was dark, except for the light of the full moon and brilliant stars. There were more stars in the Red Woods than Danny had ever seen. He wished Mrs. Contreras was here so he could show her how wrong she'd been to make him doubt himself. He would tell her that he forgave her because now he was on his way to everything he wanted. He could hardly take his eyes off it, and he reached to touch the portal. He couldn't help it. He took a step forward.

"What is that?" Danny asked. There was a flat metallic arrow sticking out of the invisible wall.

Glory sucked in an excited breath. "I'd bet my entire hat collection that it's a key. A strange-looking one but still a key."

"Is that what's keeping the portal intact?" Danny reached out his hands. He was a key and a glass portal away from being closer to seeing Pili again.

Before he could get any closer, a hooded figure moved through the forest. It darted straight for them, the end of the cloak flapping like a superhero in flight. For the briefest moment Danny considered: What if that figure running through the woods was Pili?

"Pili!" he called out with a booming voice.

"Danny, wait!" Glory tried to pull him back. "I don't think that's—"

But Danny was already reaching for the metal key that separated him from the Red Woods. He went for it. It felt like sticking his hand into an ice bath before a great force pushed him back. He couldn't move farther, and the shimmering space exploded into a brilliant, blinding light. They all shouted as a great blast of wind knocked them on their backs.

"Are you all right?" Auntie North shouted.

Danny's head was spinning. The glass tube that once held the parchment was shattered on the ground. When he sat up, the sheer portal vanished.

"It's gone!" he cried. The doorway was gone and so was the metal piece that had been wedged there—like a key. Danny slapped his hands on the ground to possibly find where it fell. There was a sharp *plink*, but he couldn't see where the sound had come from. "Where is it?"

"Danny?" Glory called his name. Her voice was so full of fear that it made Danny whirl around. Glory and Auntie North gathered beside Danny. There was a thumping sound that he couldn't place. It took Danny a moment to realize what he was looking at.

A creature stood on the path in front of them. Danny searched his mind for a name for the creature. He had the body of a gray hare and was as tall as Danny, but the great antlers that sprouted from his temples made him appear much taller. A cloak was tied around his throat with a shimmering green jewel, and a leather belt was slung across his chest.

Jackalope.

The creature was a jackalope! A very angry one who stomped on the ground and lowered his antlers, ready to charge.

←14→

The Jackalope Prince

THE JACKALOPE THUMPED HIS great furry foot, ready to attack. The ends of his long cloak flapped in the breeze. His antlers were dusted with a gold powder and as they leveled with Danny's face, Danny thought it was the last thing he'd ever see.

But as the jackalope charged like a bull, so did Orion.

The very brave pup leapt, and his nose barreled into the jackalope's chest. The two of them rolled and tumbled off the side of a nearby stone bridge and down into the stream. There were barks and grunts and a great big splash and a scream.

"Orion!" Glory shouted. She ran without thinking, and Danny followed behind her.

When Danny climbed over the boulders, he knew where the scream had come from.

Orion was safe. He'd climbed out of the stream on the other side of the bank and shook his entire body.

The jackalope, on the other hand, was having a difficult time. Now that he was no longer trying to attack them, he didn't seem so threatening. In fact, he needed help. The jackalope thrashed in the shallows. His cloak was soaked through, and his gray fur was darker now that it was wet.

"I'm drowning!" he shouted. "You've all killed me! That's what you've done. I hate water. It's a very terribly nasty thing."

Glory was kneeling on the side of the stream. She held a fallen branch and shouted, "Grab on!"

The creature cried out, "Why would anyone cover themselves in something so *wet*?"

"I'm trying to *help* you," Glory said, though now she sounded frustrated. "Take hold of the branch."

Danny fought the urge to laugh. The jackalope was in only a foot of water and he wasn't even moving anymore. He was splashing his short arms and furry legs.

"Stand up!" Danny shouted.

But the jackalope would not listen. He writhed and cried. Danny was certain someone was going to come and discover them. It was one thing to excavate a stone from the archway, but how were they going to explain a five-foot-tall rabbit with golden antlers?

"He's not listening," Glory said.

"Excuse me, Mr. Bunny!" Danny shouted.

The jackalope went rigid. He was so still that for a moment, Danny wondered if he'd gone into shock.

He had, in fact, gone into some sort of shock. The jackalope shot up to his great paws. The left one thumped three times, causing more of the cold stream water to splash on them.

"How *dare* you," the jackalope said, puffing up his chest. "I am not a *bunny*! I am a jackalope. Do *bunnies* have great, magnificent antlers such as these?"

Glory gave a little shrug and jittered behind her hand. They didn't want to laugh *at* the jackalope, but she couldn't help it.

"Bunnies do not have antlers," Glory said.

"*Magnificent* antlers," the jackalope corrected her, and hopped onto the bank where Danny and the others stood.

"What should we call you instead?" Danny asked.

"I am Llewelyn the Fifteenth, Prince of the Red Woods," he said while wringing the water from his long scarlet cape. He had shorter arms, like a kangaroo, but not as tiny as a T. rex.

"Well, Llewelyn the Fifteenth, Prince of the Red Woods," Glory said. She stood up straighter but still wasn't as tall as the creature. "You owe us an apology."

"I owe *you* an apology?" The young jackalope prince smacked his paw on his chest.

"Yes," Danny said. He pointed at the ground. "When you came through, I dropped the key."

"I am worth one million keys!"

Orion barked a response.

Llewelyn turned to the pup and scowled. "Absolutely not. *You're* the reason I nearly drowned."

"You can understand him?" Glory asked.

"Of course," Llewelyn said. "Don't you speak Wild?"

"Wild?" Danny asked.

"That's the language of all creatures, except humans. Though I do speak Human quite well."

"I don't think we're going to get that apology," Danny whispered to Glory.

"I will not apologize," Llewelyn said, and crossed his

arms over his chest. "As prince of the Red Woods, I command you to send me back. What is this place? Why have you brought me here?"

"We didn't bring you anywhere!" Glory said.

"We're trying to get *into* Rio Luna," Danny tried to explain.

"Are you a witch?" Llewelyn gasped and shrank like something was flying at him from the sky. "Or worse! A shadow?"

"No! We're just kids," Danny said. "Why would you think we're shadows? I thought they were all banished."

The prince sucked in a tiny breath, then glanced around suspiciously. It was as if he was afraid something was going to attack him from thin air. "Because there are whispers in the realms that the Shadow Queen is gathering her forces to wage war on Rio Luna once again. A jackalope prince can never be too careful in these matters."

Danny didn't like the sound of that. If Rio Luna was in trouble, then so was Pili. He rummaged in his pack for a picture of his sister. Mrs. Contreras had used a really old kind of camera that printed out pictures right away. He handed the picture to the jackalope, who only glanced down at it but did not take it. "Have you seen a human girl in your land? She looks like this, but she'd be two years older now."

"There are dozens of human children in the Red Woods," Llewelyn said, though he still seemed upset. He walked over to a boulder that was lightly covered in moss and sat down as if he were holding court. "I can't know all of them."

Danny stared down at the tops of his sneakers. So far, meeting a creature from other lands wasn't what he'd expected. This bunny was mean. Sorry, this *jackalope* was mean. He was spoiled and rude and reminded Danny a little of the Garner twins.

Auntie North cleared her throat, appearing behind them. "I think it's best if we sent our royal jackalope back to his home. It'll give us another opportunity to look for Pili there."

"We can't," Danny said, fearing how the jackalope would react at hearing this news. "At least, not until we get all four clues. I'm sorry, Prince Llewelyn. I'm sure you're in a hurry to go home."

"What—" Llewelyn asked, hopping around them so quickly, Danny felt himself getting dizzy. "What kind of witch can't wield their own witchery?"

"I'm not a witch," Danny said. "I'm a kid."

"What's that in your hand?" Llewelyn asked Danny, and snatched the book from him. "Ella St. Clay! That thief. That scoundrel!"

"Thief?" Danny said the word as a question. "She's a writer."

"Perhaps, but she will always be known as the person who ruined our majestic aviary to help the Moon Witch."

Danny and Glory exchanged a conspiratorial stare. They both knew that there were yellow birds and fairies in Leigh the Bard's underground home. He wasn't sure how, but they nodded at the same time. Neither of them would betray what they had seen.

"Imagine!" the jackalope continued. "We were so good to her after she found her way to the Red Woods. And how did she repay our kindness? By helping Ser Leigh the Bard release all of the birds from their cages. After she left on her adventures across the rest of Rio Luna, I had to train *squirrels* to deliver letters across the kingdom. Do you know how difficult it is to train squirrels to do anything? Not to mention Ella also stole my father's prized parrot."

"Maybe she thought she was doing the right thing," Danny said with an innocent shrug.

"The right thing would be opening up a new portal and letting me go home. This land smells absolutely horrendous."

Danny breathed in the scent of fresh flowers, the green of the park, the moss on the stones, even the hot dogs from a nearby stand. But beneath all that, there was also the exhaust from cars and buses. Still, Danny didn't think it was so terrible as the jackalope prince claimed.

"It smells like smoke and iron. There's hardly any magic in this land. I can barely catch a whiff of it." Llewelyn's nose flared in Danny and Glory's direction. The jackalope stomped his foot so fast, it looked like a blur.

Danny thought about what Pili would do. Once, she'd protected Danny from a nasty bully at one of the homes they'd lived in. Because he was bigger and stronger, she decided to offer him pieces of her chocolate. It turned out, no one liked to talk to him, but Pili was the one to reach out. Sure, that didn't work with everyone, but he remembered that kindness was also part of what made him worthy of this quest. Danny didn't have any chocolate, but he knew that they all wanted the same thing. To get to Rio Luna.

It was then that the sunlight illuminated an object at the jackalope's feet.

A flat gold arrow. A real one.

Danny picked it up and held it in his palm. It was a

wonky shape, but it had been wedged in the glass wall that had separated this world from the magical one. Danny was positive that Glory was right. What he held in his hand was a key, though it didn't look like it'd fit into any lock that he'd ever seen before. But he could feel the magic within it. He was sure that this was what the clue revealed.

Glory grinned widely at him. "Only three more."

"I have a better idea," Danny told the prince. "We're trying to find my sister. Here we have the first key. There are three more. Once we have them all, we'll be able to unlock the door to Rio Luna. If you come with us, we can get you home through the next portal we find. It's the only way we know to get you back. Deal?" He put out his hand.

The jackalope stared at Danny's outstretched fingers for a long time, but finally he gave the boy his paw.

"Deal," said the prince.

———

Danny was worried that a five-foot-tall jackalope might draw some attention. But the broach that pinned Llewelyn's cloak together was no ordinary thing. It allowed him to become invisible to humans once he activated it. At first glance, Danny had thought it was a gem, but up close he saw it was a gold acorn with two green leaves at the stem.

Back at the Siren's Cove, they warmed themselves in front of the fire and Auntie North brought out tea and treats. Llewelyn did not care for tea, but he was very fond of the carrot cakes.

Danny took the same seat on the couch as the night before and set the book on his lap like a comforting blanket. He'd gotten his first glimpse into Rio Luna. It had been at his fingertips. Three more to go.

Llewelyn was staring out the window and shook his head. He continued to eat carrot cakes. Danny thought the prince looked almost *relieved* about being away from home. That he could relate to. He'd been away from the Garners for only a day and already he felt happier and full of possibilities.

It occurred to Danny that Llewelyn hadn't just been on a quiet stroll when the portal opened. He had been running. What, or who, was he running from?

"Was something chasing you, Llewelyn?" Danny asked.

Llewelyn straightened, lifting his button nose to the air

like he couldn't stand the smell or sight of Danny. "Whatever do you possibly mean by that?"

"I only meant that when we saw you in the portal, you seemed scared. It's okay to be afraid—"

"I was not *scared*. I'm not scared of anything." The prince frowned. On top of that, the smell of this realm offended him. Still, it didn't stop him from enjoying another carrot cake.

Danny wanted to remind the prince that he was pretty scared of drowning in a shallow stream not moments ago, but he didn't want to embarrass him.

"Here's what I don't understand," Glory said. "How were you able to come through the gateway? Leigh said it was too small for anyone."

Llewelyn gestured at his magnificent antlers. "These can crack through most enchantments. I barely know my own strength. Oh, and by the way, my parents—the king and queen of the Red Woods—will want to know I've been taken. Do you have any messenger squirrels or birds?"

"We have mail carriers," Danny explained. "But I don't think they can get to the Red Woods right now any more than we can."

"Also, we didn't *take* you," Glory said. "You came through *our* portal."

"I guess you're stuck with us." Danny grinned widely.

The prince of the Red Woods, while having a tendency to be a little mean and bossy, could be fun to have around. Danny remembered what Pili used to say. *There was no such thing as a coincidence.* She believed that everything that happened was written in the stars. Sometimes, that thought kept him going when he began to lose hope of ever seeing her again.

"Do you believe in coincidences?" Danny asked the prince.

"Of course I don't believe in coincidences," the jackalope prince said. "That's ridiculous to even insinuate I'd believe in coincidences. What is a coincidence?"

"A coincidence," Glory said, "is something that happens by chance."

"Right," Llewelyn said, glancing from side to side. "As I said, I don't believe in that. Why?"

"Maybe we're all meant to be friends. Maybe we're all meant to help each other," Danny said.

Llewelyn shook his head, and his eyes shifted nervously from side to side. Danny wondered if the prince was hiding something. "I wouldn't go so far as to say *that*. When I sensed the portal open, I thought it was the shadows bringing their dark magic onto our land, so I ran. You know they're not allowed to enter Rio Luna anymore."

"I used to wish that a shadow would come and take me to a magic land," Danny said. "I dreamed about one the other day. Before I had proof about all this."

"Close your mind to them, Danny." Llewelyn shook his head so hard, Danny and Glory ducked so they wouldn't be hit with the antlers. "Shadows will wear your bones and skin if they could."

"Remember what Leigh the Bard told us," Glory said. "The Shadow Queen twisted the shadows for her own purpose."

"Now, Glory," Auntie North said, clearing her throat. "Ella St. Clay never gives the Shadow Queen's perspective. She's only a villain in Leigh the Bard's story."

"My queen mother has reported whispers across all the regions of Rio Luna," Llewelyn said, lowering his voice. He glanced over his shoulder, like he was afraid he was being watched. "All report seeing strange occurrences. The mushroom rings in the Red Woods shriveled up and began bleeding a gray ooze. Then every squirrel lost their fur. Something is happening, and we're not sure what it is, but I'd bet all my inheritance that it has to do with the Shadow Queen."

"When did all of this start?" Auntie North asked.

One of his ears twitched. "The whispers began about two years ago, but the other things started yesterday."

Two years ago? Danny's stomach tightened painfully. Two years ago, Pili had written her name in the same book he was holding. She had found the clues and collected the keys from the portals to get to Rio Luna. Leigh the Bard had all those protections because she wanted to do everything in her power to stop any shadow from slipping back in. What if one had gone in with Pili?

Danny rooted through his backpack. He found his space-themed metal lunch box. It was one of the few gifts Pili had been able to give him and he cherished it, even if he no longer used it for food. He kept the most precious things in it, like pink shells he'd found at the beach, ticket stubs, a race car, a stick he found that could have been a magic wand, and taped to the inside lid was a class photo from when Pili was in the fifth grade. It was a little clearer than the Polaroid he'd shown before.

"Are you *sure* you haven't seen this girl before?" Danny asked. He held up the picture to the jackalope prince.

"I told you, there are too many children in the Red Woods—"

"Please look at her, Your Highness," Danny pleaded. "She's the only family I have. I have a feeling that my sister, us, the book can all be connected to what's happening in Rio Luna. But I just have to be sure that Pili isn't in your part of the kingdom."

The prince of the Red Woods was many things. He was rude and eager. He was petrified of water, and he was greedy when it came to sweets. But the one thing he did have was a very big heart, even if he didn't quite know it yet.

He looked hard at Pili's face in the glossy photograph. Danny hoped that Llewelyn could see what he saw. In her brown eyes, there was more love than anyone could possess. He took the photo and bowed his head at Danny, who had to jump back so he didn't get poked with one of those antlers.

"I have not seen her before. I swear it on my life. If your sister is in Rio Luna, she has not been in the Red Woods. We would have heard of a human girl carrying Ella's book."

Danny remembered that time he'd thought he'd found real fairy dust and leapt off a roof, thinking he could fly. As he plummeted through the air, there was a desperate moment where he thought he could grab hold of something. Maybe Pili would materialize out of nowhere just in time to save him. Or maybe a shadow, one of the good ones, would snatch him up and carry him away. But no one did. That helpless feeling began to grab hold of him.

"However, I am a most magnanimous prince and agree to help you on your quest until I can safely get back home," the jackalope said. "When a prince makes a promise, he is bound by his word. Besides, it is clear to me that you'll never get to the next clue without my assistance."

Danny laughed, and Glory giggled. Llewelyn didn't know that the golden threads of magic came alive only for Danny. He didn't want to correct him because it felt like a victory to have the prince on their side.

Orion began barking and wagging his tail. Perhaps it was all the talk of shadows and magic, but Glory and Danny both jumped out of their seats.

"He's saying it's time for his walk," Llewelyn said. "I'll take him. It's very exhausting speaking Human for so long, and I really must stretch my magnificent legs."

As they went off, Glory walked them out and rattled off instructions to Llewelyn to stay in the park across the street.

When she came back into the living room, she threw herself onto the couch.

"Do all princes have such a high opinion of themselves?" Glory asked, blowing a stray curl away from her forehead.

Danny looked at the mess the jackalope had made on the tray and began to clean it up. "I don't know. I think that there's something Llewelyn isn't telling us."

"What makes you think so?" Glory asked.

He didn't want to say anything until he was sure. But Danny knew a runaway when he saw one. Whatever Llewelyn needed, Danny hoped they could all help one another. "I just have a hunch that we should give him a chance."

"You should always trust your hunches," Glory said. "Isn't that right, Auntie North?"

The woman was staring into the fireplace. For a moment, Danny thought that she might be crying because her eyes were so glassy. But then she smiled like all was well in the world. "That's right, my Glory. We have a lot of work ahead of us."

"I'm ready for anything," Glory said. "I just hope it's not another tree that tries to choke us to death."

Danny gulped at the memory. In those moments, he'd been too scared to really think about what was happening.

It was like when he jumped off the roof. There was desperation and fear of never seeing his sister again. He cracked open the book and concentrated.

"Call on the magic, Danny!" Glory said, nearly jumping up and down on the couch. "You already did it once."

"I have to concentrate," Danny said. His stomach felt like there were ants crawling around his intestines. He told himself it was just nerves. But now that his group of friends was growing, there were more people he could let down.

They waited for Llewelyn and Orion to return. Both of them were in a great mood after their walk.

"Just in time," Glory told the jackalope prince.

"Indeed. My contribution will be to lend an ear to the story from this velvet chaise by the far window."

"I'll go and get supper ready," Auntie North said. "I'm starting to worry you've only had sweets today."

Llewelyn raised his paw. "I happen to be a sugartarian, thank you."

Glory turned to Danny and whispered, "I *don't* think that's a real thing."

"I can *hear* you," the prince chirped. "I have excellent hearing."

Danny closed his eyes and tried to concentrate on the

same feeling as earlier in the day. He'd read the story and called on the magic until the arrows showed themselves. The sensation was there beneath his skin, waiting to be revealed.

He turned to the next story. It was called "Sinchi and the Cliffs of Nowhere." A small picture of a furry hamster was etched beneath the title. The creature was holding on to a star as they flew in the air. Danny had asked Pili if they could get a hamster as a pet, and she said, "One day, when we have our own home." He hoped that day would come soon.

"'Sinchi Victorel, the youngest son of Sapa Cuy, was star-gazing with his brothers and sisters at the top of a hill when a star fell to Earth. The siblings argued over the augury. Some said that falling stars were a sign of dark times. Other believed a star, when found, could take you on a great adventure across the skies. The eldest children thought it best to retreat into the homes beneath the stone temples of Ingapirca. The youngest children decided to go.'"

"I would definitely go," Glory said.

"Star-flight isn't all it's cracked up to be," Llewelyn chimed in.

Danny was starting to wonder if the prince liked *anything* at all. Well, other than sugary sweets. Danny happened to agree with Glory. He would have gone because he'd always, always wanted to fly.

"Anyway," Danny said, and kept reading. "'Sinchi Victorel, who it turned out was a guinea pig (much bigger and wilder than a hamster, but closely related), never returned home. He hitched a ride all the way to the land of Nowhere, traveling from star to star. He began to capture the falling stars and trap them in an enchanted satchel. He was going to bring the stars back to his brothers and sisters and start his adventure again.'"

"Did he?" Glory asked, sitting forward in her seat. "I can't remember."

"I don't enjoy a cliff-hanger," Llewelyn said.

"That's where the story is ripped, but I remember from when I had a copy of the book. Sinchi made it back home with his siblings and carried with them wishing stars to give to the kids in their village," Danny said, handing *The Way to Rio Luna* to Glory.

She ran her finger down the ripped page in the seam. "That's selfless and kind."

"Yes, I'd keep all the wishes for myself, if I had them," Llewelyn chirped.

Would Danny give away wishes instead of keeping them? He was sure that was what Pili would do. He didn't have any wishing stars to test himself. Instead he focused on preparing himself for what came next. The magic burned hotter than before. Danny closed his eyes and thought of Pili. Of riding on shooting stars the way the guinea pig siblings had done. Pili was his connection to this strange, new, wonderful magic he was beginning to understand. This time, he found the magic within him a little easier, but it was not easy to hold on to. Kind of like the way Orion liked to run away on his leash. Danny latched on and pulled. When he looked down, he was holding on to a golden chain made of light. At the very end was a small spearhead.

"Whoa!" Danny shouted. The chain was attached to the center of his palm. "What is this?"

"I think that's a pendulum," Glory said. "They're used to keep time, but witches use them to search for things like spirits or people. Map! We need the map."

Glory grabbed the map of New York they had used earlier. Danny held out his hand over the surface and nearly fell backward. The pendulum swung wide. He closed his hand into a fist, the magic was like holding on to a lightbulb that was still on.

"I think we're going to need a bigger map?" Danny said.

Glory grabbed for one that showed the whole world. Llewelyn gathered close and Orion tried to leap up to the table as if he could get a better look. Danny let the pendulum fall and it spun and spun and spun. Then the spearhead darted near the equator. It punctured a little hole in the paper, and a single word came alive with that familiar golden script. *Ingapirca.*

"Sinchi's home!" Danny said. The pendulum vanished into a puff of golden shimmer. "It's real."

Llewelyn tried to pronounce it a couple of times and got it on the last try. "Ing-ah-peer-kah?"

"That's down in South America," Danny said. He turned to Glory with worry. "How are we supposed to get there? Look at how far away we are. We'd need to be able to fly! I only have six dollars in my lunch box."

But his friend did not seem worried, not one bit. Glory was grinning, her eyes alight with the same kind of mischief he had seen in the Moon Witch. "Did I mention Auntie

North was an archeologist who traveled the world as part of her job?"

Danny nodded.

"Pack your bags, Danny Monteverde and Your Royal Highness!" Glory said. "We're going to Ecuador."

←15→

The Way to Ecuador

AFTER WHAT FELT LIKE a dozen phone calls and arrangements, Auntie North got in touch with friends at an archeological site near Ingapirca. Glory packed her favorite clothes and shoes. Danny was given his own pick of the litter, which included a beach-green shirt that said AHOY! He decided to wear it right away. Danny found his passport in the lunch box where he kept all his valuable things. It was hard to imagine the small baby in the photo as himself, even though all the information was correct. Had his parents planned to travel with them so young? He'd flipped through the empty pages countless times, but none of them had a stamp. He wished he could tell his parents that he was going to do the one thing they had planned on. Where would they have gone? Pili would throw out names like Puerto Rico and Greece! Human places, to be sure, but at least they would have been together.

The following morning, Danny was ready before anyone else and waited nervously for the others to come down. Auntie North was ready last, to Danny's surprise. She was dressed in slim beige pants and wore a blazer over her white blouse. She called a taxi for them, and they crammed into the back seat. It was a good thing Llewelyn's acorn brooch kept him invisible, because he stuck his head out the window the whole time, shouting, "What great metal trees this realm has!" And Orion wagged his tongue right beside him.

They arrived in Long Island at a small airport with an empty security line and no other passengers. Auntie North shook hands with a man in an orange safety jacket. The fellow had dark eyes that, for a second, completely covered the whites of his eyeballs. Then he blinked, and Danny realized he was seeing things. Was he that nervous? It was only the biggest mission of his life.

As they loaded their bags into the cargo hold, Danny noticed it wasn't the kind of airplane where they'd get flight attendants and movies. There were giant crates marked FRAGILE tied down and stacked neatly.

"These are going to the museum down in Cuenca, Ecuador," Auntie North said.

They all strapped in, and Auntie North handled the business with the pilot. As they took off, Danny and Glory held each other's hands. It wasn't her first flight, but the way she practically bounced in her seat told Danny that she was excited.

He gasped as the plane lurched forward, ready for takeoff. Glory squeezed his hand. Llewelyn let out a nervous laugh and spoke to Orion in Wild.

There was a moment of weightlessness, as if the ground had given way beneath him. It quite literally had. He was *flying.* Sure, it wasn't the way he'd expected. He was inside a metal plane instead of hitching a ride with a shooting star. But he was *in the air.* Thousands and thousands of feet from the ground. It was a very different kind of magic. His nerves even began to unravel the way the arrows had. He had a clear direction. But just as he began to drift off to sleep, a loud yell shook him awake.

It turned out there was another thing Llewelyn the Fifteenth, Prince of the Red Woods seemed to be afraid of, and that was very great heights. Though he was strapped in tightly by various belts across his torso and lap, the young jackalope still shut his eyes and wailed as the plane shook and rattled during a small thunderstorm.

For Danny, it was the greatest feeling he had ever had. When they lived in New Jersey, there had been a local fair in the grounds behind a church that Pili had taken Danny to. He only remembered flashes—fluffy pink cotton candy that melted on his tongue, hundreds of lights flashing from the rides, music flowing from a nearby stage. Danny was too small to go on the one roller coaster, but at least they got to go on the carousel and teacup ride, where they could spin themselves over and over again. Flying filled him with the best memories. That was, until Llewelyn began talking.

"We're going to die, aren't we?" the prince asked. "We're going to plummet right through the clouds and fall to our certain dooms. It's not normal, this flying business. Flying is for birds. I miss my aviary, though now the birds only stop by to eat their fill and drink and don't talk to me at all. How high are we?"

The prince rambled on and on until he worked himself into so much excitement he literally shut down and fell asleep.

"Is he going to be okay?" Glory asked Auntie North.

She was reading the newspaper and didn't seem bothered at all when there was turbulence. Her perfectly styled bun was never out of place. "Think about what he must be going through. He's in a strange land with strange people. It is a terrible thing to be away from one's home. Besides, judging by his snoring, he's quite all right. Brains are like any well-oiled machine. If it overheats, it needs to cool off."

Glory and Danny nodded. She was strapped into the chair right beside Danny, and Orion had to be held in a large cage, though he had a perfectly comfortable bed and bowl of food.

"Auntie North," Danny said, "why do adults stop believing in magic? Even the ones who visit Rio Luna and then only remember their time there as dreams?"

"I haven't," she said. She closed her paper and folded it over her lap. "I've spent years researching enchanted worlds, trying to get back to the one I visited. But growing up is difficult, sad business. Everything becomes more important. I wish I could have avoided it."

For a moment, she gazed toward the small window on the freighter door. Then she picked up her newspaper and kept reading.

Danny felt a sharp thrill in his belly as the plane went through a patch of clouds. He didn't mind the shaking at first, but now it was making him dizzy. A few days ago, he was in Staten Island, trying to avoid getting noogies from the Garner twins. Now he was soaring through the sky. He had friends. He'd met a prince. The world was full of infinite possibilities and nothing, not even the turbulence of the plane, could bring down the hope in Danny's heart.

When they landed, Auntie North helped them all off the plane and onto the tarmac of a small airport. The sun was setting behind the brilliant green hills of the Andean country-side. From the top of the airport, mountains undulated for miles in what appeared to be a patchwork of land. The farthest place he'd ever been to was when his class went to a science museum in New Jersey. Now, just planting his feet on the ground, Danny's world felt bigger.

Danny breathed in the mountain air and stared at the bright orange sun setting between mountain peaks until the memory was burned in his mind. Had Pili stood in this same spot? If Danny had flown here with the help of Auntie

North, how had Pili done it? It wasn't like an orphan girl from New York City could book passage on her own. There was the old-fashioned way, which was walking. Maybe that's why Pili had been gone for so long. He'd heard of kids walking thousands and thousands of miles to try to get to a new, better place.

Before they'd left, Auntie North had hired a car service. The driver waited for them at the airport. She was a stocky woman with long black hair braided down her back. She took their bags and loaded them up in the back of a pickup truck. Llewelyn chose to ride in the truck's bed with Orion. Danny didn't own very many things, but Auntie North had managed to fill his suitcase with clothes for the journey. Everything else, like the book and the key, he carried in his backpack.

They drove from the city of Cuenca to an area called Guapan. Sweet smoke from small houses on the side of the road filled the open windows of the truck.

"What exactly *is* Ingapirca?" Danny asked as they zig-zagged on the winding mountain roads.

"It's the ruins of an ancient Inca city," Auntie North said. "There's an archeological site there. While you four search for the next missing page, I will remain at the museum to lend any help I can."

Danny and Glory rested their arms on the ledges of the car windows. He was glad that she'd never been to Ecuador before, either, so they could experience it together. The roads were cut right into the sides of cliffs. Some parts swerved in wide arches where they couldn't see another car coming around the corner. But the driver maneuvered like it was her sixth sense, especially when the clouds hung so low they would touch them. Danny breathed in the humid air, and he and Glory both stuck their tongues out to try to see what clouds tasted like. He was only a little disappointed that it was like getting face full of cold steam. When he was little, Pili used to tell him that clouds were like floating marshmallows and tasted sweet. For a short stretch, they were completely surrounded by them. They couldn't see the road or the hills. But then, after a little bit of rain, the clouds cleared and brilliant green valleys spread before them, dotted by tiny houses.

After two hours of long swerving roads, they checked into a tiny hotel with a sprawling garden and pond. Everything was made of wood, and brilliant green trees lined the property. The driver had mentioned that there weren't four seasons in this region the way they experienced in New York, and Danny was grateful the people of the hotel had extra wool blankets for them. While they waited for

Auntie North to get their rooms, Danny and Glory warmed up inside. There was a roaring fire right in the middle of the hotel dining room. Around the hearth hung black hats that seemed to be popular with the locals. Danny wished he could have one for himself, but he'd have to think of that later on. He could add "first time in a hotel" to his growing list of new things.

"You can try one on," someone said behind him.

There stood a woman with two black braids and a dress stitched with a rainbow of colors. Danny admired the colorful necklaces she wore. Each one seemed to have hundreds and hundreds of little beads.

"Really?" Glory asked, bouncing on her toes.

They went for it, taking turns playing dress-up. Danny couldn't remember the last time he'd laughed so much, especially after he tried on a hat that belonged to a baby. It sat on his head and made him feel like a giant.

"You really like playing dress-up," Danny said. "How come?"

Glory fashioned a deep purple hat with a wide brim on her head. Her two French braids ran down her back. When she looked in the mirror, Danny noticed the way her smile tugged down at the corners.

"My mother, actually," Glory said. "She loved clothes. She was a designer for an opera. I used to be able to go to her dressing rooms and try everything on. If I can't be special enough to keep the magic from the enchanted book, then I can still dress like I belong in Rio Luna."

"You are special enough, Glory," Danny told her.

Glory wrapped her arms around herself and glanced down. "I couldn't figure out the Moon Witch's challenge. I froze! Before that I stopped being able to see the arrows on my own. It's like the book picked me and then changed its mind."

Danny tried to think of the right thing to say. Whenever he was upset, Pili would be the one to comfort him. Maybe he should keep playing pretend. Maybe they could go outside and explore the pond. He decided that if he were in Glory's shoes, he'd want to hear the truth.

"You believed in me. You've never put gum in my hair or tripped me while I was walking or stolen my lunch money. Believe me, you're special in my book."

"Thanks, Danny," Glory said. He knew she was back to her old self when she picked out a blue hat with a white feather tucked into the band.

The hotel innkeeper returned. She helped carry their bags to separate rooms. For a moment, Danny thought she was staring straight at Llewelyn because her mouth was a perfect round circle of surprise. But if she saw him, she must have convinced herself that she was imagining things. How many times did Danny try to talk himself *out* of the things he saw? Shooting stars with figures riding at the tail end, animals talking to each other at the park, even the golden arrows that had led him to the book. He had to trust his gut, like Glory had said.

"Right this way," the woman said, and led them through a wooden archway lit by warm yellow light. They passed a chicken coop, and beside that a pen for fat guinea pigs. Danny thought of Ella St. Clay's story about Sinchi Victorel. Could he be the guardian? Why was he doubting that it could be true, too? He was traveling with a *jackalope*.

"Get a good night's rest," Auntie North told them.

"What about dinner?" Llewelyn asked. "You can't expect me to starve."

"There's a meal waiting in your rooms," Auntie North said. She didn't seem like she was ready for sleep. Danny wondered if she had to go to the archeological site right away.

Llewelyn yawned loudly. "Where is my room, dear Lady North?"

Their guardian's eyes went wide. "My sweet prince. You're sharing with Danny and Glory."

"Sh-sh-share?" the prince asked.

"Yes, Your *Highness*," Auntie North said. "We are part of a team. Do you have a problem with that?"

It was very clear that Llewelyn the Fifteenth, Prince of the Red Woods did have a problem with sharing a room. But he must have been too tired to complain, and so, he followed them inside.

There were three twin beds with dozens of red and black pillows piled high. A small fire burned in the corner, and two hot water bottles were laid out on top of the beds.

Danny shivered in the bathroom at first. But then he noticed how the arrows on his arms began to heat up. Were they adapting to him, or were they trying to keep him from freezing? Either way, he was beginning to grow used to the sight of them and wished he could keep them, even if it was just to show Pili. He changed into his pajamas and crept back outside. This hotel was so quiet that he could hear every creak of wood floorboards and the cry of night animals and insects. Glory didn't seem bothered and fell asleep instantly as Orion climbed to the foot of her bed for extra warmth.

The moment Danny returned, he discovered Llewelyn tucked into his own bed. There was only one pillow left for Danny, and his hot water bottle was gone. Even the sandwiches had been completely eaten, with only the pickles left behind.

Llewelyn's eye blinked open for a moment, but he shut it right away when he realized Danny was watching him. He pretended to snore.

Danny was too weary to complain, but he knew he had to speak to Llewelyn in the morning. If they were going to share rooms during this quest, Llewelyn was going to have to respect Danny's things. He wasn't going to repeat his experience with the twins ever again. "Good night, everyone," Danny whispered, and then turned off the light.

The jackalope prince answered with a real snore.

———

In the morning, Danny woke to find that someone had tucked an extra pillow under his head. Llewelyn, Glory, and Orion were nowhere to be found, but Danny could hear laughter coming from downstairs. For the first time in so long, Danny hadn't had trouble sleeping. There were no shadows or whispers. In fact, he couldn't remember dreaming at all. He supposed that was a good thing now that he knew the shadows were up to no good.

Danny picked out a fuzzy green sweater and a pair of brown corduroy trousers. He took a moment to realize how different he looked in only a matter of days. His hair was a mess of dark curls and he was still skinny as a beanpole, but his clothes fit perfectly. There was nothing wrong with hand-me-downs. The clothes he was wearing were not brand-new, after all, and he loved them. But the Garner twins would sometimes spill things on themselves on purpose just because they knew Danny would get the clothes next. He wondered how they were doing, and if they'd raised the money for their pretend-caring fund-raiser. Danny dressed even faster because getting to Pili was a sure way of never having to return somewhere like that again.

Once he got dressed, he followed the sounds of Glory's and Llewelyn's voices in the gardens behind the hotel. There was a great big tree house that overlooked the hills of the highlands and the ruins. It looked like the kind of postcard you put up in your living room or office. It would say GREETINGS FROM INGAPIRCA!

"Danny!" Glory shouted from the window of the tree house. "Good morning."

"You could wake me up next time," Danny told her. He

didn't want to come off as lazy when everyone else was already ready for the day. "I don't mind."

"I'm used to waking up at five in the morning when Auntie North does," Glory said. She ducked her head back in and made her way down the wooden tree house stairs. There was a small metal table covered in fresh fruits, breads, butter, cheeses, and hard-boiled eggs. "Auntie North already left for the dig."

"It's too bad that she doesn't get to come along," Danny said. "She's been trying to get back to Rio Luna since she was a kid."

Glory nodded and buttered a slice of toast. "She has to keep her distance to make sure the arrows reveal themselves to you. You remember what happened the other times. Being an adult must suck."

"Looks like it. Where's Llewelyn? I thought I heard him."

"I'm right here. I couldn't sleep at all because someone was snoring, if you must know," Llewelyn said, hopping down. He made a face at the beautiful spread of food. "Did you eat all the raspberry pastries, Glory?"

Glory shook her head. "No, *you* did, Your Highness."

Llewelyn looked extremely disappointed in himself.

"I pulled up a map on my tablet," Glory said, showing Danny the rendering of the area. "The ruins are less than a mile by walking. We walked farther when we found Leigh the Bard. We have to expect that it will be hidden by protective enchantments. Not to mention—a test."

Danny considered this. He pushed up the sleeves of his fuzzy green sweater and examined the arrows that shimmered on his skin. There were no drawings because they knew the location. "If Leigh the Bard was the guardian of the first key, does that mean that Sinchi Victorel belongs to the second one?"

"How cool would that be?" Glory responded. "If I were Ella St. Clay and I wanted to protect each page, what better way than to entrust each key with the one person who lived through the story!"

"There's only one way to find out," Danny said.

"But Ingapirca is so big. More than the Loch in Central Park. It could take days to search every corner for a shielded door. Though I do hope Sinchi Victorel doesn't live beneath a tree, too . . ."

Danny felt the exact same way. Glory was right. They needed to narrow their search. He tapped the arrows on his arms. "A little help, guys?"

But they didn't move in the same way that they had

when they went to find the Moon Witch's enchantment. Perhaps Sinchi's house didn't *have* magical protections. Suddenly, he had a wild, strange idea.

Danny turned to Llewelyn, who was having a conversation with Orion in Wild. *"Prince* Llewelyn, do you think you could speak to one of the furry locals and ask if they know a Sinchi Victorel?"

"Like who?" Llewelyn asked, indignant for no reason.

Glory flashed her usual grin and nodded her head toward a small pasture, where a group of fluffy white alpacas were grazing.

Llewelyn considered this for a moment. His great antlers caught the light with their beautiful leaf and vine designs. He let out a little huff, but then waved his paw in a very dramatic gesture. "Naturally. Whatever would you have done without me?"

Danny counted dozens of alpacas and sheep munching on grass. One of the ladies from the hotel gave them a wooden bowl filled with carrots, but Llewelyn ate half of them before they got to the clearing.

The alpacas were clustered in groups near a trickle of water. They had thick white wool and there were dozens of newborns walking around. Danny started to approach one when a tall daddy alpaca rose from his sleep and barred the way. There were bits of grass in his thick, curly white fur, and when he noticed the strangers in his area, he lowered his head and stomped on the ground.

"Uhh, guys?" Danny called out to his friends. "What do I do?"

"Leave it to me," Llewelyn said, and hopped in between the boy and the alpaca. Llewelyn bowed his head and waited for the alpaca to do the same.

When they spoke in Wild, it sounded to Danny like clicks and chittering. The alpaca's mouth tugged at the corners. They went back and forth, louder and louder. The dozen younger alpacas around them lowered their heads as their papa alpaca stomped on the mound of grass. Danny and Glory retreated a few steps. Llewelyn even shrank back, but only for a moment. Danny wished he could understand what they were saying because the jackalope prince was practically sweating before the great alpaca. Llewelyn cleared his throat and faced his fellow travelers.

"What is it?" Danny asked. He and Glory shared a worried glance.

"This is Yap Yap. He says he's never heard of a Sinchi Victorel."

Danny felt his stomach turn.

"But," Llewelyn said, raising his paw, "Yap Yap says that *his* father used to tell of a young guinea pig who ran away from home on a shooting star and was never seen again. He says there are no free guinea pigs in these parts anymore, but there is one who lives near the ruins. However, he doesn't like visitors and doesn't leave his home."

"Maybe he'll change his mind?" Danny asked hopefully.

Llewelyn chortled. "Clearly this fellow has never had a royal guest."

————

Glory and Danny borrowed bicycles from the hotel and rode them up and down the hills. The roads here were dusty, but because the day was bright and clear, Danny didn't mind the clouds of dust that rose up from the ground. He hadn't ridden a bike in so long. Freddy and Teddy would chain their bikes up so that Danny couldn't borrow them, even though they were in the garage collecting dust.

Now he sped beside Glory. The promise of getting the next key lit a fire in his veins. The world was green and blue blurs around him, and the future was as bright as the sun. Llewelyn and Orion ran beside them. If there was one thing the prince was very good at, it was speed. The jackalope bounded across the emerald fields, and though he was going uphill for steep climbs, he didn't seem bothered one bit. Danny and Glory, on the other hand, struggled. They panted and wheezed. It was a good thing Danny had thought to add bottled water to his survival backpack.

When they got to the ruins of Ingapirca, there was a security check for tours. Clusters of tourists gathered around their guides. There was a sign that read DO NOT SEPARATE FROM YOUR GROUP AT ANY TIME.

"Even if we wanted to take the tour and then split off," Danny said, "they'll be watching us."

"We're going to have to sneak in," Glory said.

"Too bad you don't have my charmed acorn," Llewelyn said, and tapped the pendant at his throat.

"No one likes a show-off, Your Highness!" Glory said as Llewelyn strode ahead.

They parked their bikes in a small parking lot and walked around a path that said DO NOT ENTER. Breaking the rules made Danny nervous, but he told himself they weren't there to hurt the ruins. They were there to find the next clue that would lead him to Pili.

As they walked, Danny inhaled the crisp mountain air. The clouds were hanging lower in the sky. They covered entire mountains, obscuring the small houses at the very top. From their vantage point, the ruins were neat rows of beige stone. There were so many walls missing that it looked like a game of Tetris.

He'd heard of the Pyramids of Giza and the Aztec temples in Mexico, but Ingapirca was new to him. Danny imagined what it might have been like to wake up every day and see the Temple of the Sun when it was whole. Even though it was a real place, it held magic of its own.

They made their way to a clearing where there were no tourists armed with cameras and selfie sticks. Llewelyn led the way, barking instructions. Danny hoped his gut feeling to trust the jackalope prince was right.

At the foot of a hill, under a patch of tall trees with pointed leaves, the branches had grown to make a small house.

"Please don't come to life," Glory whispered, and he could see her crossing her fingers for luck.

The house in question was simple, with a couple of stones for an entryway. It didn't look big enough for an adult person to live inside, but Danny was learning that there was more to things than could be seen with the naked eye. Across the semicircular door were signs hammered across the entire surface. The wooden boards reminded Danny of the arrows on his arms, or of intersection signs that pointed in dozens of directions. Only here it was one thing over and over. DO NOT ENTER. NO ENTRAR. It went on in a dozen languages and characters, even hieroglyphs!

"Someone really doesn't want company," Glory whispered.

"What if he doesn't let us in at all?" Danny wondered. Instead of butterflies, Danny's nerves felt like frogs jumping inside. He needed to find out. Danny took a deep breath and raised his fist to knock. He thought of Pili. He told himself to be brave like she was. The golden symbols on his skin shimmered.

But just then, before his fist came down to knock, a deep voice shouted, "Go away!"

"I haven't even knocked yet," Danny said, startling himself.

Could he finally understand Wild or was this guinea pig speaking in Human?

"I don't care! No visitors. None at all. Can't you read the signs?" Definitely speaking in Human.

Danny faced his companions. Glory was frozen in her confusion. Orion and Llewelyn chirped rapidly in Wild.

"I just have a few questions, Mr. Sinchi," Danny said.

"*Just* a few questions!" the voice said. "Everyone's got questions. What makes you think you deserve an answer?"

Danny began to tremble. If he couldn't get Sinchi to open the door and talk to them, how was he supposed to get the next key? Glory was biting her thumb nervously, and Llewelyn scratched between his antlers. They didn't seem to know what to do any more than he did. Danny thought of Sinchi's story and his journey to Nowhere. He'd cared about people once—his family. Maybe he would understand what that was like. It was worth a shot.

"I don't deserve an answer," Danny said quietly. "But if you open the door, you might help reunite me with my sister."

They waited. Danny's eyes burned from the strong wind and the threat of tears. But just as he began losing hope, the door made of sticks and vines flew open and a very large copper-haired guinea pig with glasses and a cane stomped out. There were two thick streaks of white that ran down the sides of his head. Around his neck were dozens of beaded necklaces with different symbols. There was a bright blue eye, a four-leaf clover covered in resin, a horseshoe. Danny realized they were all symbols for luck.

It took Danny several moments to recover from the shock of seeing the guinea pig walk upright and scowl in his general direction. Though was a jackalope prince easier to believe than a living, breathing creature from a story?

"Oh. Oh dear," Sinchi sighed. Danny recognized the stricken look in the guinea pig's face. Danny had seen it when he looked in the mirror. It was a look of loneliness. Of someone who'd suffered loss that had made him angry and alone.

Instead of slamming the door in their faces, he said, "Come in."

←16→

Sinchi and the Cliffs of Nowhere

THE INSIDE OF SINCHI Victorel's house was simple and tidy. There was a small fire at the center, and a hammock stuffed with grass hung on the far corner. A rainbow blanket made of alpaca hair was spread on the floor. They all had to duck their heads, especially Llewelyn, who opted to rest in the hammock hanging in the corner instead. As Sinchi shuffled around the fire with a large kettle full of water, he gasped.

"Great merciful skies!" Sinchi shouted. "You're—you're from the Red Woods!"

Llewelyn introduced himself with a great flourish of his head. He did seem to love being adored.

"But what are you doing here in Ingapirca?"

Sinchi hung the iron kettle over the roaring fire using tongs, then joined the others around the flames. Danny was beginning to realize that fires, tea, and books seemed to go hand in hand.

"I am here to aid these humans on their quest, of course," Llewelyn said. "I am *most* brave in that regard."

"Excuse me, sir," Glory said, holding up a finger. "But if you don't allow visitors, what kind of people do you allow?"

The guinea pig thought about this for a moment. He leaned against the open doorway and tugged at the short white beard of his chin, and his chocolate eyes looked up at the sky, as if an answer would simply drop out of thin air.

"Passersby. Travelers. Those who come and leave in a matter of minutes," he said. "But that was long ago. Let's see, the last traveler who was allowed to visit me was— what's today?"

"Saturday," Danny said.

"Yes, yes, that would make it two years ago." Sinchi studied Danny carefully. "Looked a bit like you, actually."

"That was my sister, Pili," Danny said, and explained their circumstance to Sinchi.

"She was a smart one," Sinchi told them. "Pretended to be a pizza delivery when I wouldn't open up. Never did get my pizza. But she was gone quickly. Said she needed to get back to her brother. That'd be you."

Danny envisioned his sister putting together the plan. He was proud that he'd made it as far as she had. Knowing that Pili had been thinking of him made him feel like he was floating.

"Two years seems like a long time to be alone," Glory said.

"It's better than the alternative!" Sinchi shouted, pointing his cane at Danny's chest. "Everyone wants to laugh in my face. They call me a deranged old gerbil who lives under the hill. I'm not even *under* a hill; I'm at the very base of it."

"Why would they do that?" Danny asked. How many times had his foster siblings called him names like *crazy* and *stupid*? They thought Danny's mind was broken because of the things he believed in. How he wished he could prove them all wrong.

"Because," Sinchi said, "I left the village when I was very little. I wanted to travel and learn how to speak Human and explore the magical corners of the realms. A whole lot of good that did me. No one believed me when I returned."

"Mr. Sinchi, we're not here to make fun of you, honest," Danny confessed. "I understand exactly how you feel."

"You do?" Sinchi said.

"I've always had a hard time getting people to believe me. They never did, and I let it get to me." Danny nodded quickly, held out his hand, and showed the guinea pig the golden marks on his skin. "That's why we're here.

"We're looking for the missing page of your story," Danny said. He unzipped his bag and brought the book out for Sinchi to see.

Danny flipped to the back, where the checkout card was. Right above Pili's name was *Justin Pierce*, scribbled in enchanted ink. It was the first time Danny truly saw those names. *Alex Guerrero. Evelyn Cho. Reina Chokshi. Damian Rizzo.* Their names had appeared when they completed their journeys. Who had all these kids been? Were they runaways too? Or did they stumble upon the book the way Auntie North stumbled upon the garden in her home? Where were they when the book chose them to reveal its secrets, that it was a treasure map to keys of an enchanted land? Did they have people who would miss them the way Danny missed Pili? The scariest thing he wondered was: Did they all come back?

"I'll tell you the same thing I told your sister. I wouldn't be doing you a favor by giving you this page."

"Please, Mr. Victorel," Danny said. "We know the dangers."

"Speak for yourself," Llewelyn mumbled from his swinging hammock.

"Whatever the test is, we'll pass it," Danny said. "I don't have anyone. I belong with my sister."

Glory turned her attention to Danny. But before she could say anything, the kettle let out a high-pitched whistle, and Sinchi poured it into a copper pot. When he saw the black liquid, Danny realized it wasn't tea but coffee. The guinea pig set out four copper cups and stuck cinnamon sticks in each, with a splash of milk and sugar. Danny wasn't sure if he was allowed to drink coffee, but Glory sipped hers politely so he did as well. It was too bitter and hot, but at least it kept his hands warm. Llewelyn asked for more sugar.

Why was Sinchi trying to discourage them from continuing on their quest? Danny thought about what Yap Yap the alpaca had said—*his* father heard of a guinea pig who lived down here alone. That meant that Sinchi was older than he looked. When Danny was little, the Finnegan family he'd lived with had a guinea pig and after a year, it died while it was mid-run on its hamster wheel.

"Did something happen to you?" Danny asked. He watched Sinchi's furry forehead wrinkle with a deep frown. "While you were over there?"

"You must understand that it was a very different time in the Cliffs of Nowhere. It was before this region had so many tourists. When I left, my kind still roamed freely across these mountains. I thought that when I left for Nowhere, I'd be back as soon as I had my fill of adventure. But I was in Rio Luna for decades. There was a war going on between the Shadow Queen and the different courts and regions. Even though I was not from there, I chose to fight against the dark with the others to save Rio Luna." Sinchi stared into the fire, like he was lost in a memory. "Did you know that shadows are *born* in Nowhere? It's the darkest part of the kingdoms. So dark you can barely see where you're going. That's why shooting stars love to travel there. You can shine brighter when everything around you is so dark."

Danny didn't have to imagine too hard about sitting in the dark. There were times in the group home when he felt like everything around him was a shadow. Not like the magical shadows that everyone kept warning him about. It was more like a heavy sadness.

"It was Ella who saved me from getting taken by a shadow," Sinchi continued. "Imagine what the Shadow Queen would have done if she'd gotten ahold of my teeth? My own pretty black eyes? Of course, Leigh the Bard imprisoned her in the mortal world and we were all saved. Ella kept on her journey and I went on mine."

"What was she like?" Danny asked. He cradled the book in his hands, open to the ripped page. It was strange holding someone's words but knowing so little about them. He hadn't thought of it that way. But the more stories he heard about her, the more he wished to know about who she was.

"Ella?" Sinchi asked. His mouth twitched like he was trying to stop himself from smiling. "She loved playing tricks on people."

"What?" Glory asked, shocked.

Sinchi laughed, not able to hold back a great big grin. Danny even saw teeth!

"After we got out of Nowhere and toward the Mermaids' Lagoons, she tricked the mermaids into thinking we were wizards. Of course, we weren't. But they left, fearing our awesome power, and we spent the whole day swimming. It was all good fun. She always marveled at the world while writing in her journal. She said she was going to tell the stories of Rio Luna so that future generations could believe in magic. After I went back home, I asked her if she wanted to come. But she wasn't ready to return."

"Wait a minute," Glory said. "If you came back home, how did Ella ask you to be a guardian of a missing page?"

The guinea pig set his cup down and used his wooden cane to help himself up. He went to the other corner of his house with the roof thatched with leaves and the walls made of deep brown clay.

"Strange magic Ella St. Clay wove. She came looking for me. I said I would do it on one condition."

"Unlimited sweets?" Llewelyn suggested.

"A ride back to Rio Luna?" said Glory.

But Danny looked around the tiny house. He shared it with no one. He didn't allow people in. It was the sort of home for someone who lived in that same dark Danny had felt when he and Pili had to be split apart. He didn't have a word for it, but he knew that Sinchi, as angry as he appeared, was mostly sad. "You wanted a happily ever after."

"Very perceptive. Right you are." Sinchi chuckled, and it

reminded Danny of a faulty radiator. "You see, you only know a version of my story. A false ending. One that Ella wrote for me as payment for my services."

Danny remembered Leigh had said something like that.

Sinchi settled in and cleared his throat. "When I was a boy, I found a fallen star. It was sunset. I was angry with my family because they always gave me the worst of the chores. I wanted to have some fun. What I never told anyone was that I had wished on a star earlier that day to take me anywhere but here. Far away, where I wouldn't have to see them. When the star fell and I had hold of it, it whisked me away to Nowhere."

"My cousin vacationed in Nowhere once," Llewelyn whispered, but stopped after a cutting look from Sinchi.

"Nowhere was everywhere I wanted. I learned to travel on shooting stars the way humans here ride on horses. I fought in the great battle for Rio Luna, and when we won against the Shadow Queen, I got back on my star and went to the Forever Gardens."

"But you did come back," Danny said. "How?"

"A star, of course. Once you catch a star or even a shadow, the trick is to not let it go. It has to take you where you ask. I even tried to bring some stars home so my brothers and sisters could have their own adventures. But when I got home, decades had passed. My family was completely gone. I heard from others they'd been captured by humans in my absence. Now I live up here, alone."

"Then why is your home not protected by enchantments?" Glory asked.

"Follow me," Sinchi said. They filed out of the house and into the great flat lawn covered in tiny white flowers and a couple of rocks. "My house isn't. No one visits the *cuy* from Nowhere anymore. But that doesn't mean that the key isn't protected."

Danny strained his eyes. Glory cocked her head, but she didn't see it, either. Llewelyn hopped back and forth, shouting to Orion in Wild. Sinchi tapped his cane on the ground and gold stones rose from the earth; they assembled in twisting rows all around Danny. Glory reached for him, and even Llewelyn tried to leap to grab him, but a force field shoved him back.

"The missing page is in there, Danny," Sinchi said. "You just have to find it."

←17→

The Boy and the Labyrinth

FOR A LONG MOMENT, Danny didn't move. He watched the walls close in around him and shut him off from his friends. He pressed his hands to the large bricks that had appeared in neat rows and turned this way and that. The stone was warm to the touch, which made him think it was the same kind of magic that he carried in his arms.

"Come on," Danny whispered to them. "A little help?"

He focused on the pull of magic the way he had other times. He was getting better at controlling it. He wasn't sure if it was because he was in dire straits or because he was beginning to understand that the magic was there for him. He'd been shy at first. He believed, he did. But he'd spent so much time trying not to that it was so easy to second-guess himself. He didn't trust what he saw with his own eyes. A long arrow with feathers at the end rose brighter on his forearm.

Danny shouted a victory yell. He knew that the arrows gave him what he needed in order to find the keys. But he didn't expect them to take any shape his mind willed. He picked up the arrow from his forearm. It stung like a sunburn. Danny knew magic came with a price. He considered throwing the arrow on its own, but how far would he get? Mr. Garner had told him he was a terrible football player.

I need a bow, he thought.

The image appeared on the surface of his left hand. It was exactly the kind he imagined Robin Hood using. The moment he removed it from his skin, the bow expanded three feet. Danny had never shot an arrow. He'd never done a lot of things, like met a real witch or heard a jackalope speak Wild. He'd never flown before, or left the country. He'd never had cinnamon coffee inside an ancient guinea pig's house. But he believed, and of one thing he was sure: Magic ran on belief.

He nocked the bow in place and pulled. When he let it

go down the narrow gold brick path, the arrow left behind a shimmering trail.

Danny ran.

Every corner turned in a twisty new direction. If he hadn't had the arrow leading the way, he would have been in this labyrinth forever. He remembered what Leigh the Bard had said would happen if he failed. He'd be swallowed by the roots. As the brick walls grew taller, he knew he would be entombed inside the labyrinth. His chest hurt from breathing hard, and his head spun from the sharp lefts and rights. Danny was just about to wonder if he was lost, when the path opened up into a circular room. Above him the bricks were stacking together, blocking out the sun.

In front of him were two pillars, and on top of each pillar was an open box. One held the roll of parchment he knew to be the missing page. The other was something he recognized when he smelled it. Sweet and shimmering. *Stardust.* The star was encased in a glass orb, spinning in place like it wanted to get free.

Danny approached the pillars. The shadows around him loomed, each brick sealing his fate. Deep inside him, he knew that if he took that shooting star, he could tell it where to go. It'd take him to Nowhere. Hadn't Sinchi said that a star and a shadow were supposed to take you anywhere once they were captured? What would Pili do? She wouldn't abandon her friends. Llewelyn had no other way home, and Rio Luna was just as important to Glory as it was to Danny. Auntie North had dedicated her life to finding a way there. He *couldn't* be selfish. Danny understood now: The choice he was faced with making was the same one Sinchi had to make. Sinchi had to change his story to get a happy ending because he made a choice that stripped him from his family. Danny was already apart from Pili. But she'd been trying to get back to him, and he knew, with his friends at his side, he had a better chance to see her again.

Danny heard his name being called out. There was only a square of blue up above. Danny gripped the wooden box with the parchment and held it tight.

Before the last brick could slide into place, the enchantment fell to the ground in a shower of light.

He held the box over his head, ready to greet his friends, but they were shouting at him and waving their arms. They were waving them forward. But he wasn't sure what he'd done wrong. It was then that a howling wind appeared, and though it was daylight outside, the ground around him was suddenly covered in darkness.

He could finally hear what they were screaming: "Shadows!"

"Run!" Glory shouted.

Danny threw himself on the ground as a freezing cold went through his shoulder where the shape of a hand tried to grab him. He kept the box against his chest as he rolled over and ran as fast as he could.

"Follow me!" Sinchi shrieked.

They ran down a slope and directly into a maze of the Ingapirca ruins. When Danny looked up, two shadows had taken the full shape of people. They flew over them and ahead, cutting them off. Sinchi slapped his walking stick in the air.

"Don't let them grab you," the guinea pig said. "Once they have you, they can wear your skin and you cease to exist."

"I like my skin just where it is, thank you!" Glory shouted.

They ducked under the Temple of the Sun, but the shadows surrounded them on either side.

"I thought you said this place was enchanted!" Danny bellowed.

They climbed over the side and kept going. The shadows sounded like the whoosh of a vacuum. The closer they got to him, the colder his body felt. Even the magic on his skin faded.

"They're breaking the enchantment," Glory said. "How is that possible?"

"Only one person has that kind of power," Sinchi said. He was nearly doubled over. Danny helped him stand, carrying him on his shoulder. Sweat poured down Danny's back. One shadow landed in front of them. It was like looking at the night sky, pitch-dark. He couldn't even see through it. They scrambled back but there was another.

"I won't let you take us," Danny shouted.

But the shadows moved closer, bringing with them their freezing cold and howling sound.

Then a great thump resounded though the valley. It was faster than any drum. Father than the way Danny's heart was beating. Danny *knew* that thump. He'd feared it the first time he'd heard it, but now he'd never been so thrilled as he watched Llewelyn the Fifteenth, Prince of the Red Woods lower his antlers and charge at the shadows that threatened them.

"Out of the way," Glory said, and yanked Danny and Sinchi from harm's way.

Llewelyn's golden antlers blazed. Each leaf, star, and arrow etched into his antlers had been given to the jackalope prince through magic. Only that would work. He barreled into the two shadows. The antlers grabbed hold of the shadows and twisted them around like taffy. Sinchi did say that once you have hold of a shadow, it has to do your bidding.

The shadows writhed and kicked and punched at the air. The sound they made was like a faraway scream. It made Danny's skin crawl. He shuddered to think that he'd once wanted to catch one and befriend it. Leigh the Bard and Sinchi were right. The shadows were dangerous.

"Don't let it go!" Sinchi shouted. He still lay on his back, trying to recover from the shock of running around so much. His glasses were askew on his nose, and he breathed heavily. "It can't stay here. We have to return it to its prison in Nowhere."

"Will it take very long?" Llewelyn asked, his eyes skyward at the two shadows trapped on his head. Danny didn't imagine that could be comfortable. "It's just, I can't see with them thrashing about."

Danny tried not to laugh, because the jackalope prince *did* save them. He was so close to losing the missing page. He kept the narrow wooden box tucked under his arm.

"Do shadows speak Wild?" Glory asked. "Perhaps we can communicate with them."

With Danny's help, Sinchi was able to stand. He stretched

out his back and neck. They could all hear his bones pop with every stretch.

"Shadows have no language," Sinchi said. "Come, let's get back before we are found. Humans can be just as dangerous, and I do not have an enchantment to make me invisible."

They trudged up a slope, then coasted down another. Each of them kept looking up at different intervals to make sure they weren't being followed.

"This proves that the Shadow Queen is free," Danny said, frowning. "And she's coming for us."

"But why would she take the missing page before it revealed the key?" Glory asked.

"You carry more than one key, do you not?" Sinchi asked. He rested on his cane heavily. "Perhaps she is simply trying to keep you out."

"Llewelyn said that there were strange things happening in the Red Woods," Glory told the guinea pig.

The prince darted ahead quickly. "I did say that. But I told you: It's just rumors."

The wind blew chilly on their cheeks, and they walked back to the pasture in front of Sinchi's small home. Orion barked at Llewelyn to make sure he didn't bump into anything. Danny and his friends walked in silence. Glory was shivering now.

Llewelyn had managed to get the shadows into one large shape so now it looked like there was a bird's nest stuck in his antlers.

"We should release the second key," Glory said. "Before more of them come."

"We can send the shadows back to Nowhere," Danny said, remembering the conditions for the gateways between the worlds. "A shadow is not a whole being. It could pass through the rip."

"Smart boy. I'm glad you chose well, Danny," Sinchi whispered to him. "I know it couldn't have been an easy decision. But you showed your kindness, something I wish I could show my family once again."

Danny couldn't imagine leaving his friends behind. How would he introduce them to Pili otherwise?

"It's too bad you can't go back through the portal," Glory told Sinchi.

The guinea pig chuckled and gripped his cane tightly.

"There's no adventure left in these old bones. Besides, who will help the others like me who get captured?"

Llewelyn's head snapped up, and they all took a step back to avoid the antlers. "Yes, I remember asking what all that was about and being rudely ignored and then interrupted by these shadow beasties. Who captures you?"

"Humans," Sinchi explained. "They capture my kind."

"Guinea pigs?" Glory said.

Danny remembered seeing the guinea pigs at their hotel and the alpaca saying that there were no more of them running free.

"We are a delicacy in this region," Sinchi said. "As long as these ruins have been here, the people capture and eat guinea pigs—or *cuys*, as they're better known. Every day more and more get caught and raised to end up in barbecues."

"WHAT?!" Llewelyn roared. Could jackalopes choke on hairballs? When he gathered himself, he continued. "That's an outrage! Where are these captured guinea pigs? I will rescue them all."

"Focus," Danny reminded Llewelyn. "You said you wanted to go home, remember? Let's get the key first."

→236←

"You could try to get back using your antlers," Glory suggested.

Danny might've imagined it, but Llewelyn appeared to be upset. Orion barked and Llewelyn responded in a series of chitters of Wild. Sinchi, who spoke the language, gave a casual shrug.

"Perhaps." Llewelyn lifted his nose in the air and sniffed. "Besides, I *should* get home. Who's been training the squirrels in my absence? My mother will be worrying. And we don't *eat* guinea pigs in the Red Woods. We're all vegetarians, mind you."

"I thought you were a sugartarian," Danny chuckled.

"I can be two things! Besides. My cousin's wife on my mother's father's side is a guinea pig princess. When I tell them all about this—*humans*." The prince gave a shudder.

Danny took a few steps closer to Llewelyn. He rested a hand on the prince's shoulder. "Thank you for saving us. Let's get put this page back where it belongs."

"Be ready to get the key after Llewelyn goes through," Sinchi said.

Danny opened the box once more. The shadows writhed, like they could sense that magic, but they were safely trapped in the enchanted antlers. Danny unfurled the piece of parchment. It was as thin as an autumn leaf. The gold ignited around the black ink, and Danny read those chosen words out loud: "'Beware the place where shadows rise.'" He lined up the ripped edges of the page, and the golden thread appeared to stitch it back together. The arrow appeared. It was a bronze color this time with a slightly longer head.

Llewelyn backed up. He wasn't much for goodbyes and so he bowed cordially and got ready to jump. The air thickened with magic and a seam came undone right in front of them. It was the size of a kiddie pool and the space within it rippled like light on glass. Nowhere was dark and full of stars. But in the distance, Danny could hear the deep wail of imprisoned shadows.

"Now!" Sinchi shouted.

Llewelyn broke into a run. His scarlet cape fluttered behind him in the wind, and in that moment Danny was convinced the jackalope would make an awesome superhero.

But Llewelyn did not go through the portal.

He stomped his feet firmly on the ground. Instead of jumping, he swiveled his head and with a thrust of his antlers, cast the shadows back through the portal. One they were through, Llewelyn grabbed the metal key wedged in the portal and presented it to his friends. Then the ripple in the air stilled and the one way to the Cliffs of Nowhere was shut.

Everyone stared at the prince, who had so complained and proclaimed that he wanted to go home.

"I have decided," Llewelyn said, brushing a tuft of hair back, "that you are all in great peril and require my royal assistance after all. Therefore, I will stay and see you through the rest of your journey. *Then* I will gladly return to the Red Woods."

He handed Danny the key. The copper metal was etched with curling symbols. It felt heavier than it looked. Danny didn't admit it out loud, but their little team felt complete with Llewelyn. This quest had brought their group together, and they were so close to the final two keys.

"Thank you," Danny said, tucking the arrow into his pocket.

Llewelyn waved his paws, like it was no big deal. But Danny could tell that it was.

"All this excitement has me famished," Sinchi said. He

led Glory and Danny back inside. Llewelyn said he needed to stretch his neck after exerting his body defeating the shadows.

Sinchi made another pot of coffee. Danny was starting to like the flavor. He and Glory gathered around the fire and ate a salad made of heirloom tomatoes and orange blossoms. He knew that if Pili were in his shoes, she would have done the same. That didn't make missing her any easier. He consoled himself with the new adventures he could share with her.

"I can't wait to tell Auntie North about this. I—" Glory began to say, when a loud screeching sound interrupted. For a second, they feared more shadows had appeared. Danny wasn't sure if they had strength for another attack so soon. His heart spiked to his throat when he realized they were missing someone. Where was Llewelyn?

———

The moment they ran back out the door, they were greeted with a brilliant sight. Hundreds of guinea pigs were running across the green hillsides. Confused humans scratched their heads and could do nothing but watch as a mysterious branch with a piece of red-and-black fabric that looked remarkably like the pillowcases from the inn waved in the air.

Llewelyn ran in front of them, shouting, "Run to freedom, my kin!"

←18→

The Way to Rio de Janeiro

AFTER A LONG DINNER with Auntie North, Danny, Glory, Llewelyn, and Orion huddled close in the tree house overlooking the hills. Auntie North looked a bit peaky and gray because of something bad she ate. The high altitude wasn't agreeing with her. But she cheered up when they reenacted their fight with the shadows.

"You were all very brave," Auntie North said. "You will need that for the next challenge. I will make arrangements and meet you bright and early."

Left to their next task, Danny could feel the day's adventure had worn him out and tested his strength. As the sun set in splashes of purple and pink, Danny didn't worry that the shadows would come back. Llewelyn was with them. He'd chosen Danny and Glory the way Danny had chosen to remain with his friends. More than ever, he was sure he was on the right track. With the keys safely tucked in Danny's backpack, they opened Ella St. Clay's storybook.

"Why don't you try reading it, Glory?" Danny suggested, offering the book to her.

Glory frowned at the hardcover in front of her. It was like she was afraid of it. "Because you know the enchantments won't reveal themselves to me."

What did Glory have to fear? She made friends with him when he had no one. She took a chance on Danny. She was on this wild adventure with him and wasn't hiding. Being brave was easy. But being brave and compassionate, that took more.

"You're the bravest, kindest of us all."

"I beg your pardon?" Llewelyn interjected.

"I mean the bravest, kindest human of us," Danny amended, to spare the prince's feelings. He turned back to Glory and held her hand. It was trembling slightly. "You believe, I know you do."

She shook her head. Curly wisps of hair were coming out

of her French braids from all the running. "The book chose you. It doesn't matter if I believe or not."

Even though he'd only known her for a short time, Danny had grown certain that Glory was just as special as he was. She was a splash of color in their day. Her light radiated from her. He hated seeing her full of doubt. But he couldn't push her into doing anything she didn't want to do. That was like the time Danny wasn't ready for swimming lessons and Freddy shoved him in the deep end. To everyone's surprise, Danny was a natural at it.

"All right," Danny said, turning the pages. Together they leaned against Llewelyn's body for extra warmth, and Orion was curled up at their feet.

———

Ella St. Clay's third story was called "The Kohlrabi King and the Forever Gardens." The first time Pili had read him the story, Danny had started drawing flowers all over the place. There was a closet in the group home that had bright pink roses drawn in crayon. He wondered if she'd ever found the gardens.

"'Long ago, in the Forever Gardens, there was a beautiful young prince,'" Danny read. "'Born with the power of the earth, he could cultivate anything he wanted. When he planted seeds, great vegetable gardens grew. Where he planted mushrooms, entire toadstools were reborn as great as boulders. Even when he cried tears of happiness, his tears turned to crystal flowers. For he was the future king of the Forever Gardens . . .'"

Danny smiled as he turned the pages. He loved this story, yes, but as he read, the enchantment did a curious thing. The arrows became flowers blooming on twisting vines. He could never get tired of magic because it kept changing. It made Danny wonder, *Is the magic changing or am I?* In a matter of days, he felt different. He felt loved and brave. He felt like he could do anything. The gloom that usually clouded his mind was banished by the light of the magic on his skin. Perhaps it was because they were huddled in one great ball, the golden flowers spread from his arms to Glory's shoulder and Llewelyn's fur. One fluttered off his skin into powder—not powder. Flower pollen. Orion chased it around in circles until it disappeared.

"Whoa," Glory said in a low, awestruck voice. She

watched the magic pass her skin, and there was only a wince of sadness when it was gone. She turned smiling brown eyes to him. "Keep reading!"

"Right . . . Let's see. 'The young prince fell in love with a human boy who traveled across the land. The prince gave up his claim to the throne even though it infuriated his parents, and returned to the human world with his love, and created a new world for all the people of Rio Luna who never quite fit in.'" Then he came to the ripped page.

"It's lovely, isn't it?" Glory said. "We keep reading about people who went *to* Rio Luna, but this is someone from there who came here."

"Why not stay there?" Danny wondered out loud.

Bad things could happen anywhere, but in Rio Luna there was magic. For Danny and Glory and countless other kids, it was a dream they could escape to when their real world didn't have room for them. But what if the opposite was true for those who lived across the lands?

Danny remembered the good moments he'd had here. Mrs. Garner, who was so quiet and so shy but always had a kind word for him when she found him crying. She baked him a birthday cake, and the two of them ate it themselves when Mr. Garner and the twins were at football practice.

Then there was Mrs. Contreras, who never lost hope in Danny, no matter what mistake he made. The Haydensons, who gave him his very first bedroom. He couldn't forget Glory and Auntie North, who had taken him in and believed in this journey they shared. His adventure wasn't going to start once he got to Rio Luna. It would continue.

As night set in, that goodness he was feeling unfurled even more with the vines and arrows.

"You don't suppose the inn has a map, do you?" Danny asked.

Llewelyn snapped his paws. "What about your portable live mirror?"

Glory snorted. "You mean my tablet? Can magic and technology mix?"

Danny shrugged. "We've seen stranger things."

Glory tapped her fingers on the screen and pulled up a map of the world. Danny held out his fingertips and let the vines flow from his skin and onto the screen. The surface seemed to glitch at first, like a channel that was scrambled.

Danny felt his opportunity of seeing his sister slip away. That was the thing about hope—you had to make sure you held on tight. But then the whole image turned golden. It zoomed in until they had an address. Danny let loose a breath he'd been holding.

"'House of Kohlrabi,'" Danny read. "'Seventeen Rio Bonito Way, Rio de Janeiro.'"

"I've never been to Brazil," Glory said.

"Can we get there?" Danny asked. He'd never imagined he'd go to one country outside the United States, let alone two. The world was so intimidatingly large, but a single book had connected it for him.

Glory nodded confidently. "We'll update Auntie North first thing in the morning."

Then the three of them yawned. So comfortable and warm as they were huddled together, the trio fell asleep just like that. Even though he'd almost been a leather jacket for the shadows earlier, Danny never felt safer.

For breakfast they ate fruits and fried empanadas stuffed with salty cheese and covered in crystal sugar. Danny had already spilled coffee on his sweater and would have to change. His flop of black curls was growing like weeds, but he didn't mind it. Glory managed to look perfectly put together as always.

Her smart blazer showed off her book pin, and her sneakers were covered in sequin-like mermaid scales. Her hair that morning was half up and half down. On the top were two neat buns that reminded Danny of Pili's favorite TV show, *Sailor Moon*. The bottom half was loose and curly.

Glory told Auntie North everything that had happened the previous night. She spoke so fast that her aunt asked her to repeat herself.

"Rio!" Glory squealed. "How exciting, isn't it?"

"You wouldn't happen to have another archaeological site in Brazil, would you, Auntie North?" Danny asked. The day was warmer, so he was in a lighter jean jacket covered in patches. Beneath that, his arms were covered in flowered vines and arrows.

Auntie North smiled, but her eyes were dark for a moment. A trick of the light in the sunny room. She seemed to be doing much better that morning. "No, but I do have a friend who owes me a very big favor. I once found him a golden parrot statue for his aviary."

"Did someone say parrot?" Llewelyn said, then he wept into his empanada.

Danny patted Llewelyn on the back, but it didn't help much.

"Auntie North!" Glory said. "Last night some of Danny's arrows rubbed off on me. I think we might have been wrong—I think—"

Auntie North leaned forward gently. She placed her hand on Glory's cheek. The innkeeper had even let her keep one of the hats she liked the most.

"Now, my Glory. What did we talk about? It's all right to not be able to see the arrows. Let Danny have his moment."

Danny watched as the smile fell from Glory's face. He found it strange that Auntie North would discourage her like that. Glory *could* see the arrows. He was sure that she could also reveal the enchantment. He wanted to say something, but he couldn't explain the tangle of thoughts he was feeling.

"Yes, Auntie North," Glory said, decidedly less energetic than before.

"Now, let's get to the airport, shall we?"

———

The second airplane ride was quieter than the first, but Danny's nerves felt like the time Freddy and Teddy cracked the TV in half and all the cables inside sparked and frayed.

Auntie North gave Llewelyn chamomile tea to calm his

nerves, and he fell asleep before takeoff. Danny stared out the window. This plane was a small jet with a golden parrot painted on the side, and they weren't the only passengers. Danny watched clouds drifting by. He made shapes out of them—a dragon. A whale with hands. A giant riding a unicorn. He wondered if Pili still did that when she looked at the sky in Rio Luna.

Glory was beside him, reading *The Way to Rio Luna*. Auntie North sat in the row across. She had her sleeping mask on, and Orion, because he was smaller than most dogs, was curled on her lap.

"Are you okay?" Danny asked.

"Of course," she said. "I mean, those shadows were scary. I don't know what we would have done without Llewelyn."

"No coincidences, remember?" Danny reminded her.

Glory settled back in her seat. "When I was little, I thought I could see shadows."

"Why didn't you tell me?" Danny shot up to a stand. He wondered if Pili had been able to see the shadows, too. Maybe she didn't tell Danny to protect him. "I would have believed you."

"Because it was just like the arrows. I could see them for a little bit."

Danny sat back down and lowered his voice. "I hate to say this. But I think your aunt is wrong."

"Auntie North is never wrong. She's the only person who cares for me." Glory wiped at her eyes. "Sometimes I'm afraid that Auntie North is right. That the reason the book didn't reveal its secrets to me was because I'm too . . . normal. Too practical. I want to go to Rio Luna for the wrong reasons. I'm not enough."

"That's not true," Danny said. He squeezed her hand. "Look at Sinchi. He ran away because he was mad at his family. Leigh the Bard found the rip in the sky by accident. If the book reveals itself to kids who have hearts that love and souls that are kind and minds that believe, then you are one of them. Trust me. I'm an expert on magic now."

That made Glory laugh. "Thank you, Danny. You're my best friend, you know that, right?"

"You're mine, too." He reached for her hand. He would prove to her that she was just as magical as he was. He shared the vines of his arms onto hers. Some kids had friendship bracelets. Danny and Glory could have friendship arrows.

When he closed his eyes, he fell into uneasy sleep. Danny dreamed of shadows who swallowed the stars right out of the sky. He dreamed of Pili, too. She looked a little bit older, which of course made sense, because he hadn't seen her in so long. But the strangest part about seeing her in his dream was that she looked right back at him. It felt like they were together wherever she was.

You shouldn't be here, little brother, she said to him just before she jumped into a sea of clouds. He tried to reach for her, but when he slipped through the cover of clouds, he was in the Sea of Nowhere that Sinchi had talked about. It was like floating inside a black hole. There was nothing, just him sinking. Then he realized the sea wasn't a sea at all, but a mass of shadows waiting to break free.

Danny started awake, covered in sweat. When they landed, they were in Rio de Janeiro, Brazil. Danny and Glory changed into shorts because the weather was warmer. Though he decided to keep the jean jacket. There was something about it that he'd taken to liking. Patches covered the entire back panel with moons, rocket ships, skulls, alien heads, and something that looked like a chupacabra. There was even embroidery that said TEXAS FOREVER on it. Danny wanted to be the first one off the plane and hurried up to the front, where the flight attendant let him off. The airport, like the one in Cuenca, was small. This one was tucked away in an area where private jets and small puddle jumpers landed and took off.

He breathed the humidity in the air. It felt like being in a cloud, just like in Ingapirca but with a more tropical view. From this vantage point they had a glimpse of the sea and the jagged mountains in the distance. It felt infinitely bigger than the place they had just come from, like the sky was wider. He'd never been much of anywhere, but he was starting to sense how every place had its own personality.

Auntie North led them through the busy crowds, her long skirt swishing around her ankles. She carried with her a binder stuffed with papers and riffled through them until she found the one she was looking for. "Here it is. The car will pick us up in the city center."

They stopped at a restaurant and filled up on *pasteles*, delicious pastries stuffed with cheese and meats. Danny drank a whole container of mango juice, his fingers sticky with the sweetness. He didn't even know you could *make* mango juice. As he ate, something new caught his eye. People were dressed in the vibrant hues of the rainbow. There were vendors selling shaved ices topped with condensed milk and creams. Women sold animal balloons. Auntie North relented and bought one for Llewelyn for his bravery in freeing the guinea pigs in Ingapirca. Because he'd activated his invisibility brooch, it appeared as if a rabbit balloon animal was floating on its own.

"Mãe!" a little girl shouted from the busy street crowd, tugging on her mother's arm. But the girl wasn't pointing at the balloon. Her clever brown eyes were looking straight at the jackalope prince, and he bowed to her with a dramatic flourish.

"How come she can see you even if your brooch is on?" Danny asked him.

"That little girl still believes in magic and her heart is true."

Danny caught Glory's eye. He wanted to say, *See? I'm right about this.* But he didn't want to do anything to upset Auntie North after she'd been so nice to him.

They wove quickly through the busy crowds. The streets were so busy that Glory held on to her aunt's hand, while Danny kept close and held Orion's leash. It was so warm that sweat dripped down the back of his neck. It didn't help that the arrows and vines on his arms were already warm. Knots formed in his stomach in anticipation of finding the third key.

He was getting closer to Pili. What would his first words in two years be to her? He should start preparing his speech.

Then a terrible worry wormed its way into his thoughts. What if she didn't recognize him? He'd grown. He'd changed in more ways than one. But he was still her Danny, wasn't he?

Auntie North pulled him out of his thoughts.

"There should be a car waiting for us," Auntie North said, craning her neck. She drummed her fingers on the surface of her papers and her frizzy hair was coming undone from her usual tight ballerina bun. Danny hadn't ever seen her so disheveled. She was starting to remind Danny of Ms. Esposito. "Now, remember. You must be on the lookout after what happened in Ecuador. We don't know what to expect from this Kohlrabi place."

The van pulled up. It was completely covered in painted parrots on the outside, and only one among them was gold. This made Llewelyn extremely bouncy. The driver of the van was an older, dark brown–skinned woman with a head full of gray braids that made twinkling sounds when she moved her head. She introduced herself as Marla, and she ran a side business dropping off passengers while she cared for the Rio Wildlife Conservatory, run by Auntie North's friend.

In the car, Auntie North chatted with Marla in the front seat. Danny couldn't understand Brazilian Portuguese, but he liked the musical sound of it. They drove right along the coast, and just as they had in the mountains of Ecuador, Llewelyn and Orion kept their heads out the window, soaking in the sun and sky. This time, Glory and Danny joined them.

When Danny was sure he had swallowed a bug, he sat back inside and tugged on Llewelyn's fur.

"Excuse me," the prince said, climbing over them to get to his seat. "My fur is very royal. Please have more care."

"Sorry," Danny muttered. "I wanted to ask you if you've ever been to the Forever Gardens?"

"Once," said the jackalope prince, "when I was a youngling. My father, the *king*, loved the parades. The king and queen of the Forever Gardens are famous for them. Out of all the Lands of Rio Luna, the Forever Gardens are the ones you go to have the most fun. That's why my mum never let me go back. She said it would get in the way of my studies. Not that it matters now since I'm here."

"Why not?" Glory said, her brows knitting in confusion. "You're still going to go back."

Llewelyn looked out the window and didn't answer for a long time. "Right. Yes, of course. I suppose this Kohlrabi King is the person we're after."

"It is his story," Danny said. "I wonder if Ella changed his ending the way she did for Sinchi."

"Of that, I cannot say," Llewelyn said, then returned to hanging out the window with Orion.

Danny thought about endings a little longer. Was it better to write a different one simply because it was happier? Wasn't it better to tell the truth? If he and Pili had never been separated and never put into the System, would Danny have ever known magic was real? Then again, why not go further back? If his parents had never had a tragic accident, then who knows what kind of person he'd be. The possibilities made his head hurt.

After an hour and a half, they arrived in front of a house nestled in a bright green hill. They hurried out of the van and approached a tall gate made of thick wood, with large turnips hanging from the corners. The sparks reappeared in the air, telling them that they were in the right place. Bright red and orange flowers surrounded the initials *O. O.*

Loud music could be heard from within the property. Laughter echoed from all sides, and farther out into the backyard.

"Is there a party?" Glory wondered out loud.

"Naturally," Llewelyn said. He brushed the fluff between

his ears back and puffed up his chest a bit the way he did when he wanted to seem grander. His tail was shaking as he waddled. "I love parties."

"Excuse me," a group of children said behind them. They were small and carrying empty baskets. They seemed to know exactly where they were going because they simply pushed open the gate and walked right down the gravelly path.

"We should follow them," Glory suggested.

They marched down to the enormous house, with colorful shutters that didn't seem to match. It was an explosion of color like Danny had never seen. There was something wild about it, the way vines clung to the sides and the roof. It reminded him of the front of the Siren's Cove, only bigger and with more leaves. It was like the green was taking over.

At the house, none of the doors were locked. They walked into a large living area. To the right was an open library filled with all sorts of books.

"Oh my," Auntie North said, smiling for the first time. Her voice became more high-pitched, and she said, "I think I'll have a look here. Go on. I'm right behind you."

The others continued past a living room where kids played video games, and a dining room where more kids ate from a banquet of fruit pies and piles of soft bread and a chocolate fountain. Llewelyn nearly stayed, but his foot started twitching when he heard music that seemed to come from everywhere at once. Guitars and percussion that mingled with cheery giggles and feet stomping. Many of the kids there seemed to be with their parents. The group that had walked in before them were in the backyard filling up their baskets with the lemons from a tall, bushy tree. If Sinchi was a recluse, the Kohlrabi King was the exact opposite. He seemed to love having people in his mansion.

The backyard went on for acres and it was filled with mango trees and orange trees and cherry bushes and blueberry brambles. There were rows with tall turnips and carrots and cabbages growing from neat rows in the dirt.

"This is incredible," Glory said as they passed a tree with starfruit. The branch seemed to lower as she walked by, and she plucked it.

"How are we supposed to find the Kohlrabi King?" Danny wondered. "The book doesn't have a picture of him."

"Wouldn't he have a crown?" Glory asked.

"Actually, the royals—" Llewelyn began to say, then gasped. "Parrots!"

He ran in the direction of a great aviary filled with all

sorts of birds, and Orion ran after him. Danny couldn't be sure if Orion was encouraging the jackalope or making sure he behaved.

"There had to be something else in the book," Glory said.

"He does love arm wrestling with the woodland fairies," Danny said. Then he felt the tug on his own arm. The magic woven into his skin was alerting him. The arrows were all pointing backward, like the time Danny had tried to run away from the book at the library, thinking he was in trouble. He heard a loud sound of someone clearing their throat.

"Did someone say royals?" A tall, burly man was standing behind them. He had a thick black beard and curly black hair, which was crowned with bright green leaves and tiny purple vegetables. He wore a white short-sleeved tunic that showed off the markings on his light brown skin. Lovely pastel flowers and leaves covered his arms right down to his wrists. On his right hand, the sprigs of leaves wrapped around the top of his palm and around his index finger, where a pale violet bloomed.

Danny looked at his own markings, and they shimmered. The arrows righted themselves. Glory sidled up closer to Danny, both of them staring at the man in awe.

"Are you—" Glory began.

Despite the tall man's appearance, his voice was soft and calm. "Ah, of course. Always do forget to introduce myself, with this being my home and all. I am Ollie Oshiro, King of the Kohlrabi Court. Who are you, travelers?"

Llewelyn, done with chasing the parrot, hopped over and stood protectively in front of Glory and Danny. "I am Llewelyn the Fifteenth, *Prince* of the Red Woods. We require your help, Your Highness. From one royal to another, of course. Oh, these are my charges, Glory, Danny, and my squire, Orion."

Danny and Glory exchanged a look. Orion barked in protest of being called a squire.

"Danny?" Ollie said. The vines and petals on his skin rustled, like real flowers in the wind. "Monteverde?"

"Yes," Danny said. He took a step forward. The Kohlrabi King knew his name. "That's me."

The king pressed a large hand on his forehead. "Oh dear. Oh no. You're not supposed to be here."

"Why not?" Danny asked. He was sure he hadn't heard the king correctly. His body ran cold. He remembered his dream of falling into the Sea of Nowhere, of the moment Mrs. Contreras told him that Pili had run away, of the seconds after he fell from the Finnegan roof.

"Because she did everything in her power to keep you out of grave danger," said Ollie.

Danny's mouth was dry and he struggled to breathe. He could barely form the single word. "Who?"

"Your sister."

←19→

The King of the Kohlrabi Court

"FOLLOW ME THIS WAY," Ollie said, and turned around before Danny could ask any questions. He led them to a small grove full of flowers and bright toadstool mushrooms as tall as Danny's hip. There were old marble statues everywhere of fairy folk, and hummingbirds buzzing all around them. Ollie waved at a couple of kids who ran past kicking a soccer ball and they bowed as he walked past.

"What do you mean by grave danger?" Glory asked.

Ollie put his finger to his lips. "Not yet. We have to make sure we're alone before we can speak."

"My sister said that?" Danny asked. His mind buzzing,

the threads on his arms going haywire like they didn't know which way to point. *"How* are we in danger?"

Ollie stopped under the shade of a mango tree. He looked around, as if making sure they weren't heard.

"Pili came to me a little less than two years ago," Ollie said. "My husband and I took her in like we do so many others. She had Ella's book with her and at first we were excited that she was collecting the keys. Everyone should experience the Forever Gardens once in their life. But Pili had been running from someone."

"Who?" Danny's voice sounded far away. The thought of Pili in trouble made his stomach clench. Who could his sister have been running from?

"Who else would be after a portal into Rio Luna?"

"The Shadow Queen," Danny and Glory said at the same time. Her name felt like biting into something sour and rotten. She was the reason Danny couldn't get to Pili.

"I have to go to her. What's the next test?" His body hummed with adrenaline. He wanted nothing more than to move as fast as he had riding the bikes across the mountain roads.

"The thing is, Pili wanted to destroy the page to make sure no one could use it to complete the map."

Danny felt like the ground was shaking beneath him. His ears were ringing. It couldn't be true. He couldn't breathe. He couldn't see; his eyes were so blurry. Pili had been here in this very grove. How had she gotten all the way to Brazil? How had she spent so much time without him?

"Where is she now?" Danny asked.

Ollie Oshiro frowned, his dark eyes full of regret. "She went through the moon portal. She told me that she wasn't coming back."

For two years Danny Monteverde had wished for his sister. He'd been passed around from family to family that didn't truly understand him. The brightest parts of his days were the moments he allowed himself to dream of their reunion. Now, after flying across the world to find her, someone was telling him to turn around. Didn't Ollie understand? There was nowhere for Danny to go without his sister.

"I don't believe it," Danny said, wiping the tears that ran down his face.

"Why would she do that?" Glory asked, her voice as hurt as he felt.

Ollie pressed his lips together like he couldn't bear to

deliver more bad news. "We believed that if we destroyed the page it would stop the Shadow Queen from having the opportunity to get back into Rio Luna. Pili took the book with her, but it must not have worked because here you are with it right now. Ella's magic must have been stronger than we thought."

Danny's forearms were glowing with magic. Each arrow turned into a bird that flew right off his skin. Before the bird could fly, it shattered into dust. He could feel the magic ebbing, leaving him. Part of him crawled back into the dark corners of his mind, never to come out. Didn't Pili know that they could have faced any danger as long as they were together? It hit him, out of nowhere, the realization that he was alone again. He was alone and falling back into that Sea of Nowhere, the mass of shadows and dark.

"I'm so sorry, Danny," Glory said.

"She wants to keep you safe," Ollie told Danny. "And she wants to stop the Shadow Queen from getting back to Rio Luna. That's why we guard each key, but she was getting too close."

"Pili's my sister. I can't just leave her there," Danny said. He replayed the Kohlrabi King's words in his head like a recording. Pili had gone into Rio Luna knowing she might not be able to come back out. But there was something Ollie had said that stuck out. "What did you mean when you said that you *believed* you destroyed the page?"

Ollie pressed his fingertips together and winced. "We burned it. But it's better that I show you."

Danny was too stunned to speak. They burned a page from the book? He couldn't believe it. If he wanted answers, Danny had no other choice but to follow the Kohlrabi King inside the house. As they walked through the groves, Danny kept tripping on stray roots. His sneakers sank into the wet ground, and he felt hot and sticky. With every step he whispered, "How could you?" And a part of him truly expected her to answer.

He thought of his sister in his dream. She told him he shouldn't be there. Maybe it was more than a dream. Maybe she had gotten a message to him from the other side. If he wasn't supposed to be in Rio Luna, then where *should* he be?

It was Glory who filled the silence with questions because he was shocked into silence. "How did Ella St. Clay come to write about you in her book?"

"Years ago, I went back to the Forever Gardens," Ollie said. He perked up at the memory. The leaves pressed into his skin moved vibrantly. "There was family business I had to attend to. But I got stuck there. The royal family didn't want to let me leave. People, beings, fairies, they don't just belong in *one* place, you see. Sometimes you go somewhere and it feels like more of a home than the place where you were born. That's how I came to meet Ella St. Clay. She'd just spent a few years reveling in the parades and was ready to return home for a bit of peace and to write down all her stories."

"Does that mean Ella is in this world now?"

"Last I checked," Ollie said, tugging on his short beard. "She helped me sneak out by dressing up my cousin, the Squash Blossom Duke, to pretend to be me. My mother must still be furious. When we left the Forever Gardens and the moon portal left us in Rio, Ella went off to write her stories. She feared being discovered so she changed her name, but she used to write to me. She came here to entrust me with the third key. Then one day, she sent Pili to destroy the last page of my story and wait for her in Rio Luna. But I haven't heard from either of them."

"Why would Ella want to destroy the thing she created?" Danny asked, startled by the knowledge that Pili had talked to their favorite author in the world. His sister had lived an entire adventure without him.

The flowers on Ollie's arms shifted. It was as if they were reacting to his mood. When they slowed into stillness, Ollie said, "To protect the world from the shadows ever rising in Rio Luna again. I must caution that the road ahead is dangerous. Ella didn't want her life's work being used to let darkness back into the kingdoms. And Pili would rather have you alive and well and away from all this."

Didn't anyone understand? He was brave enough to face anything. At least, he could be if they would just give him a chance. Hadn't he proved that he could wield magic? He had a heart full of love and a soul that was kind. He believed— But didn't he believe that one day he'd be reunited with his sister? The moment that doubt seeded into his mind, the arrows on his arms began to dim.

They crossed the sprawling lawn behind the giant house. It was then that Danny noticed that for every human, there was someone from Rio Luna. There were boys with tiny horns jutting from their foreheads and hooves instead of feet. There were girls with ears that were long and pointy, and they wore flowers for earrings. A group of men played guitars and beat drums while everyone sang in Portuguese. Danny couldn't understand the language, but when he closed his eyes, he felt something stir in his heart that was close to magic.

But that feeling was snuffed out. He was left cold, sad, lonely all over again. Pili had chosen to leave him behind. When he looked down at his hands, the symbols of gold had completely vanished. There was only his usual walnut-brown skin and dots of freckles.

"Everything will be all right," Glory told him as they stepped into the cool shade of the house.

But for the first time since they'd met, he didn't believe her. Danny had a terrible feeling that something was going to go wrong. Hadn't that always happened to him? Whether it was finding a perfect family who ended up returning him like a broken gift, or a kind mother who came with terrible brothers, or simply being separated from his sister—something always went wrong.

Ollie lead them to a locked door. He fished out a brass skeleton key with a tiny kohlrabi at the end. Ollie twisted the key in the lock to the left until they heard a *click crack click*.

"Welcome to my treasure room," said the king.

Danny was about to ask why he kept it under lock and key, especially since none of the other doors in the house had any sort of security. But when he stood in the center of the treasure room, he could understand why. There were paintings of the royal family on the walls. Long couches made of velvet, stacks of old books, toys all over the place. But the most outstanding thing of all was a single wall on the far end of the room.

It was the missing page from "The Kohlrabi King" by Ella St. Clay written out on the walls in elegant blue paint.

"The ink was enchanted," Glory said, spinning around so many times she had to hold on to Danny to stop herself from becoming dizzy. "That's why you couldn't destroy it completely. Because it's magic, it simply found somewhere else to go."

Glory reached for Danny's hand, and the two young travelers found strength in each other. Maybe there was still hope.

Ollie held his hands behind his back and smiled, pleased with himself. He pointed to the painting on the walls. "These are the only things I brought over with me when I moved to the human realm."

"I don't understand," Danny said, picking up a wooden pirate ship. "You were a king in the Forever Gardens. Why would you give that up to come here?"

"It's difficult to explain," Ollie said, tugging on his beard.

"I didn't feel like I belonged in my realm anymore. I wasn't a good king to my people because I always wanted to be somewhere else. When I met Isaac and he told me about the human world, I just knew that's where I wanted to be. Haven't you ever wanted to just *go* and be anywhere but the place you're supposed to be?"

"I thought I did," Danny said, and set the ship back down. He didn't feel like himself.

"Go ahead, Danny," Glory said. "We can still get the third key if the missing page is on the wall. The magic is the same."

Danny read across the blue letters. It was a true happy ending. Ollie Oshiro used the moon portal to help other lost souls from Rio Luna start new lives in the human realm. But Danny felt strange; he felt different. It was like when the shadows had surrounded him in his dream. The dark clouded everything in his mind.

"It's not working," Danny said.

"Try it again," Glory whispered.

Danny stood as still as he could. His eyes followed the script across the wall. He thought about the day he found out Pili was gone. Mrs. Contreras showed up at his house to give him the news and he hid under the bed and read his book cover to cover. The pages at the end of the book were wrinkled from crying on them. It was the worst memory he had, and it latched onto his brain like a leech. He felt his mouth moving, but there was no joy in his heart.

"It's not working!" Danny shouted. "She doesn't want me. Pili doesn't want me."

The vision in front of him blurred again. He could feel the magic leaving him. Abandoning him. Why did everything he loved go away?

"Danny—" Glory said.

But Danny wanted to be alone. He stormed out of the room and pushed his legs to a run. He could hear Glory call out after him, but he kept running beyond the courtyard. Every step Danny took in the tall grass tickled his ankles. A couple of young fairies were stacking wood together to make a fire. Orion was chasing other dogs around, while Llewelyn was speaking Wild to the birds in the gazebo. There was a dozen of them perched all along his antlers, and he'd never looked happier.

Danny wanted to feel that again, but he was struggling. He stopped at a silver pond. He thought of how far he'd come. He thought of Leigh the Bard and Sinchi Victorel.

He thought of Pili. But the real question was, did she think of him?

He was suddenly so tired. It was like invisible hands were pressing against his shoulders. Danny curled into a patch of grass. He'd read stories of people who fell asleep for decades while the world passed them by. They woke up as old people with silvery-white hair. Wasn't growing up inevitable?

Danny Monteverde fell into a deep sleep.

←20→

The Deal with the Shadow Queen

WHEN DANNY WOKE UP, he blinked the sleep from his eyes and took a look around. The silver pond reflected the moon above. Dozens of floating orbs of light floated between the trees. It took him a moment to remember where he was. He was in Brazil, in the new court of the Kohlrabi King. And his sister was still somewhere he couldn't follow. Not without the third key.

"There you are," Ollie said, walking up behind him. For such a large man, he didn't make any sounds when he walked. It was like the grass bent and twigs moved out of his path.

"I should have known. This lake was my own favorite on days when I began to lose hope."

Ollie gave Danny a sad smile as he lowered himself to a crouch. Up close, Danny could see into his kind brown eyes. The kohlrabi crown around his head moved like the petals pressed into his arms.

"What do you have to lose hope about?" Danny asked. "You're a king."

Ollie grinned, the corners of his eyes crinkling. "Only the entire state of my people. You see, I might have left my land, but I am still caring for those in Rio Luna who come here. Sometimes fairies don't make it through the moon portal. Sometimes life in the mortal realm gets too hard—all this newness and iron. It's easy to lose hope."

"You don't know what I've been through," Danny said softly.

"No, I don't, but you can start by telling me."

Danny shook his head. He was tired of talking about what he was feeling. He'd traveled to the other half of the world in search of someone who didn't want to be found. Nothing he could say would change that. He took off his jacket. The day was too hot and his T-shirt clung to his skin.

He picked at the patch on the back. One of the rocket ships was starting to come undone where the name J. Pierce was stitched in blue thread. Why did that name sound familiar?

Ollie sat cross-legged in front of him. "I've always wanted one of those. But it's too hot down here."

"It's not mine," he said, and handed it to the king. "I suppose nothing I own is mine. Things are always borrowed or cast off. I borrowed it from Auntie North's closet."

He wondered what would happen next. If he couldn't keep his promise to Glory or Llewelyn, what would they all do? Go back to New York and live in the Siren's Cove? Never see Pili again? The thought brought a sick feeling to his stomach.

Ollie Oshiro nodded gravely; the petals on his arms moved slowly across his skin. He reminded Danny of Mrs. Contreras because he was so patient. Danny knew what the Kohlrabi King was trying to do. He was trying to get Danny to "open up." But all Danny wanted to do was be angry and cry.

"She wrote you letters, you know," Ollie said.

Danny perked up. The sick feeling loosened as he sat forward. Pili had written to him. "She did? How come I never got any of them?"

"We sent them with one of my parakeet messengers, but

they came back unopened. You weren't at the old address anymore. By then, she'd already gone to the Forever Gardens."

"Do you still have any of them?" Danny asked, a small light trying to spark in his chest. It was like trying to light a candle while a breeze was blowing. "The letters."

Ollie patted his tunic. The leaves in his arms moved gently though there was no breeze. He pulled a scroll from within his ear. Danny wondered if that itched at all.

"How did you do that?"

"Well, I needed to keep it in a safe place. I might be in the human realm, but I still have the magic of Rio Luna within me."

Danny held the letter in his open palm. He remembered the first missing page he'd retrieved in its glass case. Somehow this felt even more fragile. He used his thumb to break the wax seal and read his sister's familiar bubbly handwriting.

Dear Danny,

I should start by saying that I miss you and hope that you've got someone with you who will sneak you some chocolate after dinner. I don't know if you've gotten any of my other messages. Not exactly sure how reliable parakeets are, but don't tell Ollie I said that. You'd like him.

I hope that someday soon I can tell you everything that's happened and why I had to leave without saying goodbye. I've finally found it. RIO LUNA. Just like we dreamed it and wished it and read about it. It's really real. But you've always known that, haven't you? You're the reason that I believe in so many things. You're the reason I have to be strong.

If I know you, and I'm pretty sure I know you no matter how far apart we are, you're wondering what happened to me. I can't tell you everything. (Too many spies.) But this is what I can say.

I ran away. I'm sorry, but I couldn't stay in the group home anymore. They were talking about sending me to Texas. Away from you! When I was on my field trip at the aquarium, I got on the F train and left. I went to the library and hid there for days. No one even noticed I was there except for one person. Ella St. Clay herself.

She helped me. She does that for runaways because she was one herself. Ella gave me a quest. Can you believe that? It's like I'm a knight! Anyway, I have to close the portal in the Kohlrabi Court. The Shadow Queen is rising, and we have to make sure that Río Luna is protected. It's our only chance of being together as a family.

I hope this letter reaches you in time. I *will* find you. Don't grow up too much without me, little brother.

Pinky promise,
PILI

He read the letter two more times. Each time he processed something different. Pili had run away. Mrs. Contreras was right. But she'd done it for them. The light in his chest burst into a flame with joy, then it sputtered. Ella St. Clay had given his sister a quest to close this portal. Why this one? Why not any of the others? Danny imagined that Pili was in front of him. Her curly, dark hair and her bright brown eyes, just like his, staring back at him. She'd be a little older, but she was still *his* Pili. He held out his pinky and whispered, "Pinky promise."

Then he turned to the Kohlrabi King and said, "We have to find Ella St. Clay. She's the only one who can help."

The leaves on Ollie's arms fluttered quickly, nervously. "I've tried that, Danny. It's been a year now since I lost contact. We were supposed to reconvene, but none of her messages went through. Even the talking metal message box said it was full. I thought everything was all right but the last group of Rio Luna refugees coming through the moon portal said that there's something rotten taking root in the kingdom. I suppose I could send a few more messages to the Siren's Cove."

"The what?" Danny asked. He couldn't have heard that right.

Ollie's flower petals fluttered. "That's right, you wouldn't know this. That's the name of her house. Ella changed her name to Leanna North some time ago for her safety. I— Holy turnips, why have you gone so pale?"

Danny felt more than pale. He was numb from head to toe. The Siren's Cove was Ella's house? He'd slept and eaten there. He'd felt safe there. His thoughts were a jumble, but he tried to remember when Glory said she went to live with her aunt. One year ago. Then it hit him—the jacket he was wearing. He knew where he'd seen the name J. Pierce before. It was on the back of the checkout card with the other kids who'd been chosen by the book. What did that mean? A terrible anxious knot was twisting back in his chest.

"Glory's aunt's name is Leanna North," Danny said.

Ollie frowned. He stood up and turned his face in the direction of the main house. "I've never believed in coincidences."

"If the real Leanna North is missing, then who have we been with this whole time?"

"We need to get back inside, *now*," Ollie said. A sharp breeze curled around them, raising the petals completely off his skin and taking the shape of a cyclone. "Something isn't right."

It was then that he heard a scream pierce the air.

"Glory!" Danny whirled around.

A golden light burst from the house. It was like a dome of light, sun rays bleeding into the sky. Ollie picked Danny up and ran for it, his great steps making the ground quake. Vines sprouted from the earth and turned into slick bridges so they could slide across. The breeze full of petals aided and pushed them faster. Danny held on to the giant vegetable king's shoulders.

"Code black!" Ollie shouted as they moved. "Everybody, code black! Get to safety!"

The humans and fairies scattered, hiding under toadstools

and within the orchards. Danny's heart hammered as they went. Llewelyn and Orion followed suit, and as they barreled into the house, they froze.

"What's the matter?" Llewelyn shouted.

"Glory's in trouble!" Danny bellowed.

Orion barked and they hurtled faster and faster until they got to Ollie's treasure room. It was darker. Weak candles dotted the tables. At the center of the room, two shadows gripped Glory by her arms. She yanked and tried to bite at them. When she saw Danny, she shook her head, her eyes urging him to turn around.

To the right of them was Leanna North—or the person Danny had believed was Leanna North. In the moments he'd been gone, she'd changed drastically. The skin under her eyes sagged. The pale green color was fading into a startling white. The skin around her neck gathered in drooping wrinkles. It was like she was melting.

"Let her go!" Danny shouted. He felt helpless watching his friend struggle.

"Danny!" Glory shouted back. "She's an impostor! Run!"

Orion barked, then crouched down, ready to protect Glory.

"Lady North," Llewelyn said, and clapped a hand over his heart. "How could you?"

"You sure have changed, Ella," Ollie said, his voice deep as gravel. Danny could feel the pull of Ollie's magic from the ground. There was a tremble right beneath him as bright green vines sprouted from the ground.

"We will have none of that," the impostor Leanna North said. "Unless you want my shadows to peel off the girl's flesh and wear her all the way back to the Forever Gardens. At least you'd get your wish, isn't that right, my Glory?"

She tried to grab Glory by her chin. Glory bit her hand, and the impostor wrenched her fist away.

"I am *not* your Glory," she said.

"Now, I thought I taught you better than that these last few months," the woman said. Her voice was changing. It wasn't the cool, calm voice he'd become accustomed to hearing. It was shrill, grating like broken nails on glass. She held up a flat golden arrow. The third key. "At least you've proved me wrong. You're not as ordinary and practical as I thought. You were able to reveal the third enchantment."

"You have what you came for," Ollie said, his fists balled at his sides. "Leave the girl and go."

The woman he'd come to know as Leanna North opened her mouth and laughed. Danny could see the pool of black there. He thought about those moments when he'd thought he saw a shadow in her eyes. Now he was certain that her irises and the whites of her eyes spilled out until they were completely black.

"I don't have what I came for, Runaway King of the Forever Gardens," she said. "Tell me, Oshiro. How will you feel knowing that though all your kingdoms tried to banish me, I was too strong to be defeated?"

"We did it once," Ollie said. "We'll do it again."

"The Shadow Queen can never die! Not as long as darkness finds its way into Rio Luna."

"Where is the real Leanna North?" Danny asked.

The Shadow Queen stepped between them and Glory. "I left her exactly where I was supposed to be. Now, give me the keys, Danny."

"No!" Danny shouted. He'd trusted her and she'd been an impostor the whole time. "Why did you make Glory doubt herself? You knew she could see the enchantments. You made us think we were imagining things!"

"On the contrary, Danny," she said. "See, one must

always have a backup plan. For months, Glory doubted herself and nothing I could do could make her *believe*. Only you seemed to have that talent. I knew that once you discovered that your sister had left you, you'd be easily broken."

"I'm so sorry," Glory cried. She was no longer struggling against the shadows, but they tried to hold her up. Danny felt helpless, frozen in place. The keys were in his backpack where they'd always been. He couldn't hand them over to her. But he couldn't let Glory be hurt, either . . .

"Don't be sorry, my Glory," the Shadow Queen said.

"Stop calling me that! You're not my family. What did you do to my family?"

"They did present a problem," the Shadow Queen said. "You see, Ella St. Clay was estranged from her loved ones, but she did have descendants who remembered her. I knew that without your parents, you'd go to the next of kin. What better way to get my revenge on her than to use her very own bloodline to return to my home? I knew you had it in you all along. All the children Ella helped throughout the years. Even you and Danny are so alike, after all. You possess true hearts, kindness, and bravery. Those are the three qualities Ella enchanted the book with."

"Stop this!" Ollie roared. "They are just children."

"So was I, but no one was there to protect me." The Shadow Queen waved her finger, and the shadow, which had once been attached to her, leapt free into the air and slammed into Ollie. They crashed through the glass doors and outside. The Kohlrabi King did not get back up.

Danny's anger burned through him. He searched the room for something to fight with and drew a sword from the wall. He'd never used one before, but he'd pretended to be a knight, a Jedi, even a baseball player. All he had to do was swing with all his strength.

"Don't fool anyone, boy. You wouldn't hurt anything or anyone," the Shadow Queen said. "That's what makes you so special, Danny. Now, give me the keys or your friends will become my dessert. It has been so long since I've had a sweet treat from the Red Woods."

"No!" Danny screamed.

The shadows moved faster than Danny could blink. One moment Llewelyn and Orion were at his side. Then they were captured by two more shadows and held captive beside Glory.

"Don't do it, Danny," Glory shouted. "We can't let her get back into Rio Luna!"

"Unhand me, you fiend!" Llewelyn bellowed. He even tried to headbutt them. They were prepared this time, elongating to avoid his antlers.

"Do you know why I take young ones from this land?" the Shadow Queen asked him.

Danny's mouth felt as dry as the desert. His feet were rooted to the earth. He couldn't even move if he wanted to. His heart was beating so fast he thought it might start racing out of his chest any moment. He managed to shake his head.

"Because of their light. Their hope. Their dreams. My shadows feed off it. I would have brought all the children into Rio Luna. Isn't that what you wanted? To get rid of your sad human life."

Danny didn't want to listen. He wouldn't want that, even if it meant escaping the life he had now. It wasn't worth ruining a whole kingdom with her shadows.

"Then that wretched Moon Witch and Ella St. Clay ruined all my work. It took all my strength to return, and this time, no one will stop me."

Danny should have seen it all along. How Auntie North volunteered to watch Orion when they'd gone to visit Leigh the Bard. The arch was enchanted and the Shadow Queen did not possess her own shadow. Then, at Ingapirca, she'd vanished and returned looking worn. Llewelyn had bested her shadows. That must have worn her out. Even when they arrived, she made an excuse so that Ollie wouldn't recognize her. He would have known that she wasn't the real Leanna North.

"When I rule Rio Luna, things will be different for all of us." The Shadow Queen was growing taller, her voice like a vacuum again, a great empty space. "You're welcome to join me."

"Never!"

"If that's your choice. Hand over those keys or watch me wear the jackalope's antlers as a necklace."

Llewelyn whimpered, but he did not beg for his life. He shook his head furiously, and Danny knew how much courage that must take. Glory did not look scared but furious. She struggled and tried to step on the shadow, but that's the thing about shadows—they could take any shape. This one wrapped itself around Glory like a rope. Glory couldn't talk but her eyes said it all. She wouldn't want Danny to make the trade. Llewelyn howled into the night once before the shadows silenced him, too. With so many, his antlers were useless.

"Run, Danny," Llewelyn managed to say. "I'm not worth it."

"What's it going to be, Danny Monteverde?" the Shadow Queen asked. Her body rose above the floor; her nails grew into long and dark claws. Danny realized those were shadows spilling out of her. "Are you going to leave your friends behind the way your sister left you?"

Danny thought of the letter Pili had written him. She ran away and left him behind. But he had to trust her. He knew deep in his heart Pili only wanted what was best for him. They were each other's worlds. Danny knew what Pili would do if she were in his shoes. It was more than the four of them he had to protect. Ollie was injured. The entire house was full of kids, of fairy folk looking for fresh starts.

Pinky promise, Pili wrote. She'd left to keep Rio Luna safe. To come back for him. He felt the wind try to snuff out his belief, his hope, but he held on tightly to it. He'd never let that happen again. His belief was tied to his sister and his friends, and he couldn't let that go. Even if it meant doing something terrible. Danny dug into his bag and retrieved the arrow keys from his lunch box.

"How do I know you won't hurt them?" he asked.

"I don't think you know how negotiations work," the Shadow Queen said in her hollow voice. "You can't know, but the beautiful thing is, you don't have a choice."

Glory and Llewelyn cried out in pain as the shadows pulled on their arms and legs, like they were going to rip in half.

"You need me," Danny said. "There are four keys. You'll never get the fourth one without us."

The impostor Leanna North rose higher into the air. Her shadows were like silk ribbons tugging her higher and higher. "You're wrong. You see, the last page is a door. All I need are the three keys to open it."

Danny could see no way out. If he handed the keys over, he'd be letting a monster back into Rio Luna. If he didn't hand over the keys, Glory and Llewelyn would be hurt.

Pinky promise. He understood now how difficult it must have been for Pili to choose. To leave him.

Danny took a deep breath and said, "You can have the keys if you let my friends go unharmed."

"We have a deal, Danny Monteverde." The Shadow Queen smirked, and when she did, the skin at the corners of her mouth began to peel off. She waved her hand in the air like a knife and spoke to her shadows. "Let them go."

Free of the shadows' hold, Llewelyn, Orion, and Glory

fell to the ground, weak from the cold touch of the dark creatures. It was the hardest thing Danny had ever done, but he handed over the keys.

The minute the Shadow Queen grasped her prizes, her shadows flocked to her. It was like watching ravens take flight on great dark wings. She caught the ends of them and flew into the sky, completely out of sight.

←21→

The Way of
the Stars

As NIGHT CLOAKED THE brilliant sky, Danny sent out a wish to the first star he saw appear in the sky. It was a tiny star. If you had blinked, you might have missed it.

But Danny saw it, of course. He lay down in the grass listening to the sounds of night animals. The Kohlrabi Court was silent, waiting for their king to wake. *If* he would wake. There was another star. This one bigger. He made another wish because that was the only thing he could do that was familiar.

His wish was anything but simple. He wished to make it all not true. They had been betrayed. They had been tricked. They had been used. He wished to take away all the pain his friends were feeling.

Long after midnight, Danny, Glory, Llewelyn, and Orion sat around the grove. Ollie had been hit on the head hard. Two older fairy women brought out a pillow and blankets to make him comfortable while he was unconscious. He was still breathing, but no matter what they tried, he wouldn't wake up.

There was a soft light coming from fireflies and the bright stars above. Llewelyn made a small fire inside a circle of stones, and they warmed their hands to banish the cold. The people of the Kohlrabi Court tended to their sleeping king and held a silent vigil as they processed their defeat.

"I'm sorry you gave up the arrows for me," Glory started to say, but her voice cut off as she fought a cry.

"For us," Llewelyn said softly. Orion snuggled close to his jackalope friend and let out a sympathetic whine. "I should've done something more. I should have been faster."

"No. I'm not sorry," Danny said. He wrapped his arms around his knees. "We're a team. You're my friends. I couldn't let anything happen to you."

Glory wiped her face with her sleeve. There was a tremble in her voice. "I can't believe I've been living with the

Shadow Queen for a whole year! How could I not have noticed?"

"It's not your fault," Danny said. "You'd lost your parents. You needed family, and she took advantage of that. Me, on the other hand, I had a strange feeling, but I pushed it away because I wanted—I wanted to be part of your family, too."

"You still are," she said, and they held hands.

"Well, if it's time for confessions," Llewelyn said. "There's something I haven't told you . . . The day you opened the portal—I wasn't there to guard it. I didn't sense something wrong like I said."

Danny furrowed his brow. "Why were you there, Llewelyn?"

"I was there to find a way out. I'd heard about different kinds of portals. I was actually on my way to Nowhere to search for a falling star. I wanted to run away, and I did."

"But why?" Danny asked. "You're the *prince* of the Red Woods."

"That's exactly it!" Llewelyn cried. "I'm the prince of the Red Woods and soon I'll have to be king and rule and have responsibilities. If I ever get back home, there's going to be a battle waiting for me. Do you know what the king has to do on his first week? They have to set *sail* around Rio Luna and visit the other kings and queens and I—"

The jackalope's tears wet the fur of his face. His nose had turned a bright red, and he was overcome with hiccups.

"You're afraid of water," Danny realized.

"Water is terrifying! When I was young my best friend drowned in the Mermaids' Lagoons. I was right there and my antlers got tangled in the weeds. I couldn't save him and I was drowning, too, but my mother rescued me."

"Oh, Llewelyn," Glory said, and rested her hand over his paw. "I'm so sorry that happened to you."

The jackalope used his cloak to dab at his eyes. "When I met Ollie today, I thought everything would be well. He was king and he's able to have a normal life here in this realm. Why can't I? I simply *can't* go back. I can't face my parents. I'm the runaway prince."

"Actually, Ollie was the runaway prince first," Danny said, trying to lighten the mood.

Glory dissolved into a snotty laugh. "I'm sorry, it's not funny, but you have to admit—"

Llewelyn snorted and chuckled, too. "I guess a runaway prince is a little funny."

"Just a bit," Danny said. A part of him felt good while laughing.

"But what do we do know?" he asked. "The Shadow Queen has the three arrows. She's on her way to the door. We have to warn Pili on the other side. We have to do something."

It was then that the Kohlrabi King opened his eyes and lifted himself up on his elbows. "Well, that was a nasty tumble."

The trio descended on him with hugs. Llewelyn was particularly relieved that their friend was alive and well.

"You're awake!" Danny said.

Ollie groaned and touched his head. One of the kohlrabi buds had fallen off when he was hit, but a new one was already sprouting in its place. "What happened after I so elegantly passed out? Oh, Isaac will never let me live it down."

Danny told him everything. "And then she took off with the shadows. Where would she go? We don't have a plane or a way out of here."

"You said she took the arrows?" Ollie asked. The great big fireflies began to gather all around the king. The flowers on his skin were stirring, some lifting off as if responding to his great anxiety. "We have to hurry. There's still time."

Glory and Danny exchanged a look. "How?"

"Auntie—" Glory froze and whimpered. "The *Shadow Queen* said she didn't need us. Only the keys."

"She's only half right," Ollie said, a delighted smile curling at the corners of his mouth. "She might have the keys, but the door won't reveal itself to her until you speak the whole enchantment. Ella wrote in a safety protocol in case the keys were stolen."

"The *words* are magic, too!" Glory said as it dawned on her. "I remember the third one! 'Among the Greenest Grove at Night.'"

Danny scrambled to get his backpack for the book. There was no time to waste. The Shadow Queen was already on her way, but there was still hope that they could defeat her.

"The fourth story is about sea giants," Danny said, turning the pages.

It was then that the arrows on his arms reappeared, brighter and stronger than before. His mind was clear of doubt and sadness. He held on to the good, the memories of Pili and new ones of Glory and Llewelyn. The magic shot down his arms like comets. On his left hand appeared a long stalk with curling leaves. As he looked at it, Danny realized it was a beanstalk.

"Look!" Llewelyn pointed out. On Glory's right hand the golden symbols appeared, too. It was a giant wave.

Next, Llewelyn's antlers glowed. Two words repeated themselves across the smooth bone. They were sharing the magic.

"I knew it," Danny whispered, unable to contain his smile.

"What does that say?" Ollie wondered, squinting at the script. "I never could read Ella's handwriting."

Danny tried not to snort, then said, "Giant's Causeway."

Giant's Causeway.

"There's still time," Ollie said. "If I'm not mistaken, that's on the coast of Northern Ireland."

Danny felt a thrill of hope in his belly. Ollie was right. Moments ago he had wanted to give up. He thought Pili had left him. But reading her words and knowing that she had planned on finding him was everything he'd wanted to hear for two years. Now that he'd given the Shadow Queen the keys, it was *his* turn to find her. Just as he'd planned all along. Danny secured the book in his backpack and stood in front of his friends.

"Are you ready?" he asked.

They would find a way. They had to.

"It'll be dangerous," Ollie warned them. "But you already know that, don't you?"

"It doesn't matter how dangerous it is," Glory said, "as long as we're together."

"I hate to be *that* prince," Llewelyn said, "but we still have no means of getting to this giant's place. There aren't real giants there, are there?"

"I have a way," Ollie told them, dusting the dirt off his palms. Crickets chirped and night birds sang around them. "One of the side effects of having my magic in this land is that stars come down to the grove for a moment. They're attracted to it. Though it can get cumbersome when I'm trying to sleep, to be honest. But it's a marvelous thing."

"Stars?" Glory asked.

They all glanced around. Danny realized that what he had thought were fireflies were floating back up to the sky. *Not* fireflies. Stars!

"You must each grab hold and don't let go. Whisper the place you wish to go to and the star will give you a ride before returning."

"Just like Sinchi," Danny said, grinning so widely it almost hurt.

"I'm sorry, Orion," Glory said, reaching down to rub between his ears. "But we'll come back for you."

"He'll be safe here," Ollie said, and winked. "I'm fluent in Wild."

Danny, Glory, and Llewelyn said goodbye to their friends and grabbed hold of a star each. Danny felt the heat of the light in his palm. He soared faster and higher than ever, but he didn't let go the entire way.

The Way to Giant's Causeway

DANNY REMEMBERED THE TIME he'd fallen off the rooftop trying to fly, and now it was finally happening. Except he wasn't falling this time. He was soaring. He was unstoppable. But the best part was that he wasn't alone. The stars moved so quickly, Danny held on tighter. As he flew across the great ocean, he shut his eyes and thought of Giant's Causeway, of Pili, of the next part of his adventure. He could barely hear Glory's thrilled whoops, like she was a cowgirl lassoing a bull. Or Llewelyn's terrified yowls.

When they landed, the first thing he could hear was the sea. Danny opened his eyes. His hair was a new level of windblown, and it took him a few steps to stop himself from wobbling. But finally, he could see the bright green earth and the blue-gray crashing waves that lay ahead of them. There weren't even any houses this far out, only slick black rocks that looked like pillars leading out to the sea. He thanked the stars for their safe passage, but as his struggled in his grip, he had an idea.

"Don't let them go yet," Danny said.

"Whyever not?" Llewelyn asked.

"Can you hold on to the stars the way you did to the shadows?" Danny asked.

Llewelyn tapped his chin the way he'd seen Glory do so many times. "I believe so. Why?"

"Because right now, you're our only hope," Danny said.

"Danny's right," Glory said. "We need all the weapons we can get against the Shadow Queen."

Llewelyn bowed his head. They placed their stars on the prongs of three antlers.

"It's kind of like decorating a Christmas tree," Glory said.

"What's a Christmas tree?" Llewelyn asked. Then he looked at Danny and Glory. "I mean, *of course* I know what a Christmas tree is. But we have another problem."

When they took a couple of steps, the stars threatened to

make Llewelyn take off. It was like he was a great balloon floating away. Danny and Glory were forced to hold his paws.

Danny called on the magic within him. He wasn't sure what to expect this time. The surprise was the best part. In the palm of his hand was a compass made of light. The arrow pointing north.

"This way," he said, and led the way. It felt like his whole body was wired with an internal map, and his heart knew exactly where to go.

They were surrounded by the blue-gray ocean on one side and rocky cliffs on the other. In the distance, there were columns of stone that looked like steps. Danny thought that the green countryside reminded him of Ecuador. How could places that were so apart have things that made them feel similar? Here the wind was sharp, slapping their cheeks pink. When he felt the compass dissolve into a shimmer, they stopped.

"I don't see the Shadow Queen or her shadows yet," Glory said, fear in her voice.

"I hate to suggest this," Llewelyn said. "But we need her. We might have the door but that wretched would-be queen has the keys. She'll be furious that she was wrong."

"You're right," Danny said. By now he'd learned to trust

his gut. Danny looked for signs that the dark was moving around them, but as they reached the pillars of stone that led out to sea, nothing seemed amiss. "When she appears, Glory, you'll have to distract her."

"How am I supposed to do that?"

"You lived with her for months, I'm sure you can think of *something*. Who does she hate more than anyone?"

"Ella St. Clay," Glory said at the same time Llewelyn said, "The Moon Witch."

"I'll get working on the door." Danny flipped to the very end of the book.

The last story was called "Ella and the Sea Giants." In it she tricked the giants into giving her a special quill and ink to write stories. She escaped to the Forever Gardens, and then made her way back to the human world so that every kid could have their own adventure.

"Wait a minute. There *is* no missing page," Danny said.

They stood within feet of the crashing waves. They shivered. The icy salt wind was freezing compared to the rich humidity of Rio.

"I don't understand," Glory said. She stared out to sea. "I saw it gone."

"Maybe it was part of the safety protocol Ollie mentioned," Danny suggested.

"I remember a different story about this place," Glory said, raising her voice over the loud crashing waves. "Auntie—*she*—told it to me once. A legend that a giant built this causeway to get across the sea to fight another giant. Only when he got there, the giant was *way* bigger than he'd expected."

"What did the small giant do?" Llewelyn asked, biting his nail as they glanced up at the sky.

"He pretended to be a baby and the other giant *believed* him," Glory snorted.

"A baby?" Llewelyn shouted. "That's preposterous."

"That's one of the legends around here. Stories change everywhere, the way magic changes." She looked at the book in Danny's hand. "Ella changed ink and words into magic. She turned that into something. Remember what Ollie said? There's a fail-safe. We already *have* the door. It's in the words from the missing pages."

"I hate to be the bearer of bad news, but how will we get the keys back from her?" Llewelyn asked.

Danny thought about how close they were to getting the

thing they all wanted—to get to Rio Luna. They had to be faster, together. That was the only way they would win.

"She has to think she's won," Danny said. "We have to reveal the door. That's the only way she'll show herself."

The three of them lined up on the pillars of Giant's Causeway close to the waves, ready to face what was to come. Danny flipped through the book. In his mind he could hear the chime of the magic, like bells in his ears. He looked up at his friends, both of them radiating with the sparks of light. He might have started his journey alone, but he wasn't anymore. They shared their hope and strength and sadness.

"We should each say a line from the enchantment," Danny said. "Glory was right: We wouldn't have made it here without each other. This is our quest. Follow my lead."

"Deal," Glory and Llewelyn said.

Danny shut his eyes and thought of Glory, of Llewelyn, of the real Leanna North who'd tried to protect the world she'd once called home. Ella St. Clay herself. He thought of Mrs. Contreras, who had tried to shield him from the cruel world. Of Mrs. Garner's pancakes. He thought of the good things. The guinea pigs across the hilltops, the fairies in the grove, and flying on a real shooting star. He thought of Pili and returned her words to her. *I'll find you.*

He spoke loudly. "'The road to the Red Woods is paved with starlight—'"

Llewelyn followed, "'Beware the place where shadows rise—'"

Glory said, "'Among the greenest grove at night.'"

Danny took a deep breath and recited the final sentence from Ella's story. "'You'll find love is yet the greatest prize.'"

The ground shook beneath them, and Danny quickly shoved the book into the safety of his backpack. Stones sank into the ground and revealed a single pillar bathed in light. It was no ordinary light, of course. On the surface were three divots in the shape of arrows.

Danny wasn't sure if it was the way the temperature dropped or if it was the wailing sound of the shadows, but he could hear them before he saw them. As the waves crashed, they froze in midair. Shadows spooled from the breaking surf, and it reminded Danny of the basket of yarn that Mrs. Garner kept in the living room out of reach from the twins. Until one day, Freddy and Teddy grabbed it and unraveled it. The shadows went from ribbons unspooled in the air and gathered into the shapes of people.

At the center was the Shadow Queen.

"What clever younglings. You made it just in time to find that pesky door," she said. Her eyes were full shadows now and her voice was all wrong, like broken glass and whispers. Her skin sagged off her bones, as if the magic was leaving her and she was falling apart. The only consolation was that she was no longer wearing Leanna North's like-ness. This was a woman with salt-blonde hair and eyes as black as the sky they'd sailed across. Her skin was pale with dark circles beneath her eyes. When she smiled, she revealed sharp black teeth. "I keep underestimating you."

"Glory," Danny said nervously, waiting for her distrac-tion. But none of them were moving. They were truly frozen in place by an invisible force.

The Shadow Queen twisted her hands and commanded magic. It was different than when Ollie had done it. Instead of the flower petals on his skin, the would-be queen had her shadows traveling across her skin. She was using their power as her own.

With a wave of her hand, the ground beneath Llewelyn disappeared into a deep depression. The waves crashed and wrapped around him like arms. Llewelyn floundered as water licked at his face and closed over his eyes and nose.

"You'll never get away with this," Glory shouted. "My *real* auntie will stop you. Your story will always be left unfinished because Ella St. Clay will *never* give you a happily ever after."

"Ella can't do anything from her prison," the Shadow Queen snarled. Then she went rigid. "Or should I call it my *old* prison."

"You will lose," Danny said. "We will always keep fighting."

"Then I'll just have to remove you," the Shadow Queen said. Her face turned to Llewelyn trying to keep his head above the water. "By the looks of it, your friend won't last much longer."

Three of the Queen's shadows flew down, and each grabbed an arrow key. Danny's hands were trembling as each dark figure placed the keys into their divots one at a time. There was a loud, reverberating click. The lid of the pillar opened and revealed a shimmering, crystal-clear bean. Now was his moment.

The Shadow Queen flew to pick up the bean but the magic repelled her. She went flying into the waves. Danny felt her magic loosen. They were free of her spell. It was the break he needed.

"Come on!" he shouted.

Glory and Danny dove for Llewelyn and pulled him up to safety. Shadows writhed all around them. Some tried to grab the magic bean and exploded into shower sparks of light. Others dove for Danny and Glory.

"The stars," Llewelyn said, choking on salt water. "Any minute now. It's not like I'm drowning or anything."

Danny yanked two stars from the antlers and handed one to Glory. The skin of his palms burned from their radiance, but he only had to hold on for a little bit longer. The Shadow Queen was swimming back toward them.

"Hurry!" cried the jackalope prince.

"Remember when Leigh the Bard defeated her with her power of light?" Danny felt a smile creep up his face. "Stars always shine bright when it's darkest, and her heart is the darkest of them all."

Together, they pitched their stars right into the Shadow Queen and her remaining shadows. They screamed like the roll of thunder up and away into the sky until they were nothing but a speck among the clouds.

"It worked!" Glory said.

Danny hollered his excitement into the sea breeze. Beside him, Llewelyn shook out his gray fur and left Danny and Glory drenched. But there was no time to celebrate. Danny remembered the warning that the Shadow Queen could never truly be banished.

"We have to hurry. She might come back."

Danny held the magic bean between his fingers. It was light as air, but when he pressed it, hard as glass. Everything he'd fought for was wrapped in this moment. From the day he chose to run away and follow a magic spark to the promise of being reunited with Pili. Danny Monteverde made a wish, kissed the magic bean, and flicked it into the waves.

The sea burst with bubbling water and a thick snakelike green root broke through. They were all soaked, but at least they weren't hurt. Glory watched in awe as the beanstalk kept on growing.

"I'm sorry, Danny!" the jackalope prince shouted over the waves.

"Why?"

"Because when we met, I accused you of trying to drown me. *She* definitely tried to drown me. Now, for the love of me, climb!"

Danny held on to the first branch and hoisted himself

onto the beanstalk. He grabbed on to the next leaf and the next. He remembered the first time he tried to climb a tree because he thought it would take him to another world. He remembered when he thought he was sprinkling fairy dust onto his head and then jumped off the roof and broke his arm. He remembered every time he tried to find magic and couldn't.

But there he was, climbing the biggest beanstalk he'd ever seen, just like the one etched onto his left hand. True, it was also the *only* beanstalk he'd ever seen. That didn't matter.

Danny held on tighter because the salty wind pushed against them. He looked up. The beanstalk shot right through the clouds, where they swirled like the eye of a hurricane.

"Danny!" he heard Glory shout.

Below him, there was Glory, gripping the branch for dear life, and behind her Llewelyn.

"You can do it," the jackalope prince told her. "If I can get over my fear of water, you can do this!"

"I can't! I'm afraid of falling." Glory shut her eyes and refused to look. "This is a very inconvenient time to discover a fear!"

"You just flew across the sea on a ball of gas!" Llewelyn shouted.

"It's okay if you're afraid," Danny told her. "I'm afraid, too. But do you know what got me through this week?"

The wind tugged at the ends of her scarf. Her frown was more pronounced than ever as she shook her head. "No!"

"You did, Glory," Danny told her. "You and Llewelyn make me braver and stronger because you're my friends and you believe in me. I believe in you, too, Glory. There is so much we have to discover and it's right up there. You *have* to climb."

Glory opened one eye first. She saw Danny's face so full of hope. They had lost so many things together, but they had also found each other. She opened her second eye and took a deep breath and clasped the hand he held out to her.

Glory climbed.

Danny helped pull her up for a couple of steps, but as they went higher and higher, she was able to do it on her own.

"Uh—is that supposed to happen?" Glory asked.

Up top the beanstalk vanished into gray storm clouds. In fact, the clap of thunder was so loud no one could hear the Shadow Queen and her ribbons of dark trailing behind them.

Then Danny looked down. A slithering black shape was gaining on them from the bottom. "Guys, we have company!"

He climbed higher and higher until he reached a shelf of clouds. There, at the very top of the sky was a golden archway made of ivy. A door within the clouds.

But Danny couldn't go through until he was sure his friends were safe.

"Glory! Give me your hand!"

"Go!" she told him. She was mere feet away from him.

"I won't leave you!" Danny assured her. Their fingertips touched until finally, he could grasp her hand. He helped pull her up and then she was on solid ground.

Llewelyn was next.

"Get back here!" the Shadow Queen screeched. Her skin was nearly completely melted off. The dark light within her pulsed rapidly. It must have taken great energy to try to get back to them.

"She's got my foot! She's got my foot!" the jackalope shouted over the storm.

"Maybe it's a lucky *bunny's* foot," Danny said.

He knew it was the push Llewelyn needed to keep moving because the jackalope put all his strength into reaching

Danny up top. The prince of the Red Woods glared at his friend and said, "I AM NOT A BUNNY!"

Llewelyn sank low and then jumped higher than he ever had before.

For a moment, Danny lost his balance. He felt the great drop of the sky beneath him. He could see the entire length of the sea, the ridges of Northern Ireland on the other half. As he began to fall, he was weightless. This time he didn't have the help of a star to keep him afloat. All the air left his lungs as he screamed. It was going to be a long, long way down.

But he didn't fall. The next moment, he was staring at Glory and Llewelyn. They'd pulled him back onto the cloud shelf. They could hear the Shadow Queen screaming, a terrible wail getting closer.

Together, hand in hand, the three of them ran through the portal and inside Rio Luna.

←23→

The Long, Long, Long Way to Rio Luna

DANNY MONTEVERDE STILL BELIEVED.

After everything he'd been through, his belief was so strong that when he took his first step into Rio Luna, he felt like he was home.

It took a moment for Danny and Glory to adjust to their new surroundings as the portal closed behind them. The trees were bare and stark white as bones. They spread around them in neat rows that went on forever. Danny craned his head back to look at the slate-gray sky. It was as if a single cloud was blanketed above them, so thick he couldn't even point out where the sun was. His nose itched with the sharp scent of smoke. When he took his first step in Rio Luna, he crunched on brittle earth. Panic seized him and he turned left. There was a dry stream that snaked through a clear path of bony trees. To his right was what looked like a throne carved out of stone surrounded by bare thornbushes.

This was not the Rio Luna he'd dreamed of. The worry on Glory's and Llewelyn's faces mirrored his own.

"Where are we?" Glory asked the jackalope prince. She crouched down to look at a cluster of black toadstool mushrooms speckled with blue dots. She was about to touch one when it split open. She yelped as black liquid oozed from the open wound and a hairy white spider crept out and skittered away. Where were the fairies? Where were the silver trees that shimmered in the breeze? What about the river that was home to dozens of creatures?

"If we are in Rio Luna, I do not know this dead land," he answered.

"Maybe we did something wrong?" Danny asked, and flicked away a winged black beetle that landed on his shoulder. They all jumped back as a red snake crawled between their feet and vanished into a hole in the dry ground. He spun once again, trying to get his bearings. They'd done everything right, but here they were.

"Someone's coming," Llewelyn said, his long ear turned in the direction of the noise he heard.

Danny's insides gave a tight squeeze when he saw her. Though he couldn't see her face in the dark of the white forest, he knew. The girl ran between the trees with expert ease. She knew every twist and turn, every rock that might be in her path. She was wearing a raincoat made of clear flower petals, but she still wore her favorite Coney Island T-shirt.

Pili.

Danny rubbed his watery eyes and blinked several times, but he was not imagining it. She was different than he remembered. But of course, it was inevitable to grow up, even when one traversed a fairyland. Her dark curls were so long they were almost down to her lower back. Her light brown skin had more freckles over her nose.

He started to speak. What was he supposed to say to her? He'd spent years imagining this moment. It wasn't right. There were too many people. Too many sad eyes staring at them. He could hardly breathe. He could hardly see unless he blinked. Danny had wished so hard, but had he ever thought any of those wishes would come true?

Yes. Deep in his heart he knew he had believed.

And yet he simply stared at his sister. Where would he even start to tell her how he'd gotten there?

"I guess we're both runaways now," Danny said.

Pili ran to him, half crying and half laughing. She pulled him tight and didn't let go for a long, long time. She brushed his hair back and kissed his forehead. For the first time in years, Danny took a real, true breath of relief.

"I'm so sorry that I had to leave you," Pili cried.

"I made it," Danny said.

"I was supposed to be the one to save you, little brother." Pili pulled back and looked at him, her eyes shimmering with tears and pride. "You didn't stop believing in me."

He looked at his feet, at the dry ground covered in brittle branches. "I did, for a moment."

That's when Danny remembered they were not alone. He introduced his best friends to his sister.

"Pili, what happened here?" Glory asked softly. "Is Rio Luna safe now that the Shadow Queen is gone?"

"Far from it," Pili said, and looked around the small clearing. "Do you see this? The river has dried up. The trees have lost their shine. This is where the Shadow Queen was last before she was banished. She's going to try to come back."

Llewelyn cracked his paws. "We'll be ready and waiting."

There was something Danny needed to ask his sister now that he was finally with her. "Pili, in your letter, you said you were with Leanna North. The real Ella St. Clay. Where is she? Where did the Shadow Queen imprison her?"

Pili's face puckered with worry. For the first time Danny noticed a tiny scar over his sister's brow. What had she been through while she was here? What had she seen and done? Pili turned to Glory.

Llewelyn let out a sharp cry. "Come on, tell us! What more can you do to this poor boy?"

"Don't mind him," Glory said, and laughed for the first time since arriving. "He feels all of his emotions."

"We got separated after we went through the moon portal in Rio," Pili said. "We made it here, but I haven't been able to find her. She's not in the old prison. The Shadow Queen lied. Shocker."

"Do you think—?" Glory let herself think the worst.

"No," Pili said firmly. "I'm afraid our work isn't finished. When I heard that you were following Ella's map, I came here to wait for you."

"How did you know?" Danny asked, still holding on to his sister's hand. She was here and she was real.

Pili's features darkened. "I stole a shadow, but the power is unpredictable."

"That was you," Danny said. "All those times."

Pili's face softened when she turned to Danny. "I'm sorry. I thought I could speak through it, but I couldn't control the magic."

"What do we do now?" Glory asked.

"We rest," Llewelyn said. They all looked at him with shocked grimaces. "I mean, we have to rest. We can't fight a great evil *and* rescue a not-so-famous author, not to mention bird thief and Glory's real aunt, if we haven't slept or eaten."

"But where do we go?" Danny said.

"I have to face my parents," Llewelyn said, and bowed to Danny and Glory. "But I'm sure they'll love it when I tell them that I'm on a quest. All of this to say, my service is yours."

"I'm in," Pili said. "I haven't made it to the Red Woods yet."

Danny smirked at the jackalope. "Are you sure it's not *too* dangerous?"

Before Llewelyn could answer, a golden light shot out of Danny's backpack. He shouldered it off and retrieved the glowing copy of *The Way to Rio Luna*. Danny turned to the last page, where the enchanted ink was stretching across the lines of the checkout card. There, beneath Pili's name appeared three new ones. *Danilo Monteverde. Glory Papillon. Llewelyn the Fifteenth.*

"We did it," Danny said, marveling at the magic before them.

"We're just getting started," Pili said.

Glory grabbed Danny's other hand and it became a chain-link effect. Pili held Llewelyn's paw until they came full circle: a group of misfits ready for anything.

ACKNOWLEDGMENTS

THANK YOU ALL FOR taking the journey with me into Rio Luna. Ever since I was a little girl, I was drawn to magical stories. I loved Disney everything, and as I got older, I found the darker, scarier versions of the cartoon tales I'd grown up with. Stories change and evolve as time goes by. Fairy tales are a reflection of the societies who tell them. I've taken some liberties with some truths. For instance, I have no way of knowing if J. M. Barrie and Lewis Carroll ever went to their wondrous lands, but that's the great thing about stories: They have infinite possibilities. *The Way to Rio Luna* is a book about magic, friendship, and holding on to the goodness in the world.

The magic of this book wouldn't be possible without

certain people. Thank you to my editor, Mallory Kass, for giving me the incredible opportunity to become part of the Scholastic family. You asked the right questions and helped me dig deeper into the heart of the story. To the wonderful Scholastic team who worked on this book from copyedits to production, especially Josh Berlowitz. To Erin Maguire for bringing Glory, Danny, and Llewelyn to life with your gorgeous art, and to Keirsten Geise for the cover design.

To my friends who are now immortalized in the pages of this book as fairy-tale characters, Dhonielle Clayton, Mark Oshiro, Leigh Bardugo, Leanne Renee Heiber, and Victoria Schwab.

To my incredibly supportive family. I hope I can write enough books one day so you can each get a dedication. I'm working on it.

Finally, to every kid who has felt alone in the world. You are special. You are worthy. You belong. This book is for you.

ABOUT THE AUTHOR

ZORAIDA CÓRDOVA IS THE author of many books, including *Star Wars: A Crash of Fate* and *Incendiary*, the first book in the Hollow Crown duology. She was awarded the International Latino Book Award for Best Young Adult Book in 2017 for *Labyrinth Lost*. Her short fiction has appeared in the *New York Times* bestselling anthology *Star Wars: From a Certain Point of View* and *Toil & Trouble: 15 Tales of Women & Witchcraft*. She is the co-editor of *Vampires Never Get Old*, a YA anthology. *The Way to Rio Luna* is her first middle-grade novel. Zoraida was born in Guayaquil, Ecuador, and raised in Queens, New York. When she isn't working on her next novel, she's planning another adventure. She definitely needs a jackalope sidekick.